SKYSCRAPING

Cordelia Jensen

PHILOMEL BOOKS

An Imprint of Penguin Group (USA)

PHILOMEL BOOKS
Published by the Penguin Group
Penguin Group (USA) LLC
375 Hudson Street, New York, NY 10014

USA | Canada | UK | Ireland | Australia | New Zealand | India | South Africa | China
penguin.com
A Penguin Random House Company

Library of Congress Cataloging-in-Publication Data
Jensen, Cordelia.
Skyscraping / Cordelia Jensen. pages cm Summary: In 1993 in New York City, high
school senior Mira uncovers many secrets, including that her father has a male lover.
[1. Novels in verse. 2. High schools—Fiction. 3. Schools—Fiction. 4. Secrets—Fiction.
5. Fathers and daughters—Fiction. 6. Gay fathers—Fiction. 7. New York (N.Y.)—
History—20th century—Fiction.] I. Title. PZ7.5.J46Sky 2015
[Fic]—dc23 2014035150

Printed in the United States of America.
ISBN 978-0-399-16771-3
1 3 5 7 9 10 8 6 4 2
Edited by Liza Kaplan | Design by Semadar Megged | Text set in Winchester New ITC Std

Dedicated to my family—past & present

1993

FALL

PILOTING

I have everything I need.
My bag. My key.

The security man knows my name,
lets me in.

Soon the school will be full;
for now, quiet, empty.

Climbing stairs,
the room halfway between floors.

Just the way we left it:

A tidy stack of blue layout sheets in the corner.
Two long rulers.
Side by side.

Font book in the drawer.
White counters flank me,
like plane wings.

In the corner, the books.
In order, from year to year.
All those smiling faces.
Expecting. Believing.

I open my favorite:
1976,
the year I was born.
I spiral into their past:
girls with ironed hair,
boys in bell-bottom jeans.
Wonder who's still friends with who.
If they kept their yearbook.

Shutting it gently,

it's my time now.

I unpack:
new erasers, set them in a row,
paper clips, labels.
Take out a rag.
Wipe the layer of dust from the counter.

White can always get brighter still.
Wings after the rain.

In just two days,
we launch.

And maybe, years from now, some baby,
born today, will grow up to be an editor like me:

Someone who knows how to turn the present into memories.
Someone who knows how to capture time.

She will see our faces.
Me. Chloe. Dylan.
Wonder who we grew up to be.

Then, she'll sit,
use her own silver ruler, draw her own lines

like I'm doing now.
Taxiing just before
takeoff.

MIDAIR

In my windowseat—

midair—

spying on Riverside:

a ponytailed jogger, an old man walking a poodle,
a balcony of trees sweeping over the Big Rock,
cars breeze up the Henry Hudson,
four boats bump down the river,
Manhattan's skyscrapers dwarfing North Bergen.
Dad peeks in, giantlike, fills the whole doorframe:
his round face, his fading tan.

Mira, he says, it's time. It's a big day.

I watch New York City blaze by.
The sun almost swallows the sky.

I'm ready.

Touching the window,
the glass warm,
I leave my very own mark,
floating up, high
into
the pulsing orange sky.

TIME FLIES

Today, I'm a Senior.
My sister, April, a Freshman.
Dad pecks our cheeks,
Mom, still sleeping.
He claims she said
have a nice day.

Outside,
April hands Sam
the homeless man
a Pop-Tart tucked in a paper towel.
Dad would be proud.

Past Cafe 82, Celestial Treasures, Harry's Shoes.
Past a yellowing leaf twirling with a Burger King wrapper,
floating, then falling together, on the cracked curb.

Time flies—
once we were little girls dancing to the Go-Go's,
mirrored walls showing us ourselves,
matching long blond ponytails,
April arms out, voice open, singing loud.
Me, taking the slow part, spinning in circles.

Now, eyes locked, under the glass bus stop,
a sign reads:
In December, not just tokens only, MetroCards too.
Write it down in my planner; make sure April sees.

Our backpacks heavy with possibility,
a million taxis storm by,
blowing our hair up in this September breeze,
the bus yawns, opens its doors to us,
like it has just woken up.

OUR LAST FIRST DAY

I.

April and I sit catty-corner,
back of the bus.

Dylan comes on,
flashes his pass,
flannel heavy with smoke.
Ask if he's ready.
He shrugs at me.
I tell him I'm psyched,
he mumbles high school's wack,
I tell April to ignore him.
Dylan scored 16 billion on his SATs,
the rest of us have to work,
he sticks his tongue out at me.

II.

The bus crawls through tunnels,
lands straight on Park.
We file out,
windows above
lighting us,
so bright
we're fluorescent.

Chloe, at the corner,
somehow earlier than us,

a lit cigarette, fountain Coke,
cutoffs, Sharpie-drawn Converse,
Mother Love Bone T-shirt.
Me in a plain white V-neck,
plain blue blue jeans,
I click my brown clogs together.
Chloe and I, different styles,
friends our whole lives.

III.

April, nervous, says she doesn't want to go in.
I whisper Dad's go-to line:
let the butterflies into your heart.
Some girls from her class fly by in formation,
she picks up their wind, glides into their frame.

I grab Chloe's ringed fingers,
no more waiting, let's start—
we move from sidewalk to gates—
Dylan winks at me,
we swarm in—

our last first day.

I squint back into the sky

knowing that this is the moment

in the movie of our lives

where the prop guy

rains down

confetti.

MY INNER EYE

Adam, white cap, used to wait
inside the school lobby, his palm
gently on my back, steering me
into the school elevator
up.

Now he's at college,
not with me to celebrate
this beginning, this end.
Not here to steer me
in.

So many afternoons spent with him
at school in our Yearbook office.
Supplies in order,
all our plans
made.

So many evenings
in his beige-carpeted apartment,
yearbook pages spread out around
us.

Watching *The Princess Bride*,
sipping crushed ice Cokes,
resting gently on coasters,

working, watching, kisses
in between.

Though we aren't together anymore,
we keep in touch,
my inner eye is locked on Adam's gaze,
he's smiling at me, applauding almost,
as I make this steady, even flight
my own.

INTO SPACE

First up, Astronomy,
push in the heavy black door.

Seat by Dylan,
a game of hangman.

I guess the word, *Existentialism*,
he draws a happy face
on the dying stick figure.

Mr. Lamb projects:
slide after slide,
Earth from the moon,
blue and green swirls of beautiful.

My heart pounds:
I am inside of it.

I am part of the rotation.

Dylan passes a note,
says that he's been reading
the Existentialists,
that Senior year, by definition,
means we are in crisis:

Questioning what, if anything, has meaning.

Asks me to join him and Chloe after school
to ponder our existence.

I tell him:

        I am not in crisis.

        I am part of the rotation.

        Ask him if he's thought more
        about where to apply for college.

Mr. Lamb's voice cuts through,
Constellations aren't just pretty pictures.
I gaze at the star map,
down at my table black as night,
make sure no one sees me

as I constellate,

dotting
Wite-Out
on the table's edge:

my   sky
    own   night
         little

WHERE WINDOWS ARE STARS

Once when we were little
Mom guided us outside—

> past Dad handing "little cigarettes"
> to his friends from Mexico—
> "Gloria" shouting from the record player—

she left us on the balcony and returned to their smoky haze.

Told us to search for stars.

Sisters in matching gold-speckled party dresses
> out in the air
> a thousand blinking lights

April asked where the stars were.

I moved her hand from pointing up to straight ahead and said

in New York City, April, windows are stars.

CAPTURING TIME

For some, Yearbook meetings
are gossip sessions.

I try and organize the staff
on copy, quotes, Senior pages—

They call me a stress-case
but they don't know how relaxing
it is to cut and paste
draw boxes of ruler lines
glide a pen down
and around
smiling faces.

Give them a place to stay.

A memory design.

So that, years later,
we can look and see our faces,
stare into the past
as though looking into the night sky,
where stars that have already died
keep showing us their shine.
When our future might be up in the air,
not knowing where we will be next year,
this is the only way to capture time.

I tell them:
so much will change,
even us,
but this book
will stay the same.

Some nod, some roll their eyes,
but all of them draw
frames like plane windows
on blue graph paper,
the color of sky over water.

REAL-LIFE THINGS

Lasagna night.
We layer
noodles, sauce, cheese,
Dad asks me
if I've given more thought
to touring Columbia
(where he teaches)
before I apply early admission.
Heart races as I
imagine my dorm room,
glimpsing Dad in the courtyards,
hosting April uptown for meal plan dinners.

Say, okay, sure, maybe in a few weeks.

James,
dark eye makeup, piercings, tattoos,
Dad's Teaching Assistant and April's tutor,
eats with us
then helps April with Spanish,
plays chess with Dad.

Mom, home later after blowing glass all day at her studio.
April and I sit, discuss her new teachers,
my new staff,
spin ice cream into a sweet soup,
watch *90210*.

Dad says we should watch shows about real-life things.
Mom tries to join, asks questions about Brenda, Brandon.

I turn up the volume.

Mom eats cold lasagna alone.

TIME TO REMEMBER

I.

Later, on the phone, Chloe yawns,
she and Dylan smoked up,
says her guy is cheating on her.

Hear Chloe's nonna screaming.
Parents gone. No siblings.
Chloe tries
to smoke it all
away.

But it's Senior Year, the time to remember
everything.

II.

A long machine message from Adam
saying hi, hope I had a good first day
at school, leading my first Yearbook meeting.
Ever the editor,
offers to brainstorm
yearbook themes with me.
Says he's been pretty busy,
plans to join a frat.

Lie in bed,
wonder if he'll drink,
something we used to not do, together.

Eyes closed, listen to Dad listening to opera,
banging around the kitchen, house sounds stirred
with the whooshing cars on the Henry Hudson—
a city lullaby rushing me into easy sleep.

ON AGAIN, OFF AGAIN

In the morning, Dad gives us breakfast.
Mom   gone again,
like we're a TV family,
there at her convenience—
she can choose
when she wants
to switch us on, tune us in.

OTHER PEOPLE'S WINDOWS

Twenty Seniors chosen to mentor Freshmen.
April says she has me, why does she need them.

She opts out,
I opt in.

In a room on the twelfth floor I've never been to,
the windows here show us into
other people's lives.

Huddled around a wooden table,
Mr. R tells us congrats on being chosen,
assigns us a partner, a group, tells us
we also have to interview our own mentors.

Something catches my eye,
I peer into the windows:
TV flickering in one.
An old woman in a turban, smoking.
Curtains. A potted plant.
And a little girl staring out,
unblinking like a doll,
too little to be alone.

I raise my hand to wave but

Mr. R calls on me to share with the group.

My mentor is my dad.

I look back to the windows:

TV still flickering in one,
the woman still smoking,
but the little girl, staring out—

gone.

RECORDING SESSION

September

SESSION ONE

So, this is my dad, Dr. Dale Stewart.
He's a Spanish Literature professor at Columbia.
He's pretty smart.

> *Gracias, mija.*

Okay, Dad, so we are supposed to interview our mentors. I have a
list of questions here.

> *Shoot.*

Number one: What's the most important quality of a mentor?

> *Well, before I answer that, do you know who the*
> *original Mentor was?*

What do you mean?

> *From the* Odyssey. *Odysseus left Mentor in charge*
> *of his kingdom when he went away: Mentor watched*
> *over Odysseus's son. He did this gladly. You see, a*
> *mentor teaches for the love of teaching. A mentor*
> *leads his students, sometimes indirectly, to the*
> *answer.*

A mentor can be sneaky.

> *(Laughs, coughs)*

What's your answer to the question then?

> *I think the most important quality of a mentor is that they are open to following students where they want to go. Not always pushing their own agenda.*

Okay, got it. Thanks. Number two: Who's one of your mentors?

> *That's easy. Your mother.*

What? Why?

> *Because she helped me the most at a time when I needed it, and always encouraged me to dream big without telling me what to dream.*

She did?

> *Yes, Mira, she did.*

UNKNOWNS

In second grade, school had us
plant flowers in pots, decorate them
for our moms for Mother's Day.
I picked the flowers with the most buds.
Not sure which color to choose.
I painted tiny animals,
the only thing I knew Mom liked.
Chloe planted daisies for her mother, painted her pot blue.
Said her mom didn't like strong smells.
Everyone seemed to know their moms' favorite flowers
colors
smells.
All of them experts.

I went home, nervous,
pink carnations in my painted pot.
Dad, April and I ate dinner,
waited and waited.

Mom never showed up.

NEWBORN STARS

In the fall of ninth grade,
      Mom left a note saying she'd gone
      to Italy for a while, to study.

Mom left,
April wept,
Dad cooked,
I smashed one of her glass fish.
Buried it in the back of my closet:
mouth open,
gasping for water,
drowning in a corner, dark as sea.

Day after,
Dad held a family meeting,
April held a glass frog,
I said I didn't care that she left—
she was hardly here anyway.

After the meeting,
April stuck next to me.
I stacked my sweaters like Pez candy:
pink, purple, gray.
Assembling order from mess.

That weekend,
Chloe and I got fake IDs,

so easy
it surprised me.
I never drank,
just followed Chloe into bars,
poured my Sprite into her vodka
while she
looked the other way.
Took fake puffs from cigs
newly sprouted from her fingertips.

Newborn stars
take millions of years to form,
billions of tons of mass to make.

But the constellation of a family
can shift shape
in seconds.

TURNED

She was gone 13 months,
returned just before Halloween,
Sophomore year.
I had already found Yearbook. Adam.
When she came back,
arms full of glass,
April said welcome home,
Dad held her.

I said nothing.

She reached out for a hug

but I

turned

the other way.

MISMATCHED

Years later,
sorting mail,
bills from junk,
things Mom can't be bothered with,
I hear her fruit earrings rattling
down the hall.

She matches our apartment:
plastic oranges and bananas drip from her ears,
her lips painted red peppers,
bright like our dining room table.
Her hair a tousled salad like
laundry left unfolded in piles.

Down the hall,
Mom's artwork:
glass roosters and fish hijack the bookshelves,
infest the coffee table.
As many times as I try
to place them in cabinets
or line them in height order,
they march back in,
a disordered stampede,
a resurrection.

Mom's closet:
green scarves overlapping purple purses,

scattered costume jewelry
falling on top of random shoes, socks.

Mine: jeans, hung, creased,
sweaters folded in color order.
One pair of sneakers, flats, boots, clogs.

One mom
one daughter

mis-
matched.

SOMETHING STELLAR

In Astronomy class,
formulas scatter the blackboard.

Mr. Lamb tells us
in May we'll see
a solar eclipse as a class.
We'll all stand
in the sun
and go dark
for a minute.

In May, seven months from now,
just a month before graduation
into college, yearbook done,
a month before we're flung

into space,

I will be
        something stellar.

Even as the world goes dark around me,
I'll keep my shine,

I will not eclipse.

SHADOWING

Tuesdays, out early, two frees in a row.
Sky so blue, walk past the bus stop,
skip through the park,
the reds and yellows
nip at the greens,
tell them it's their turn to change.

Cross the bike track,
remember flying, back of Dad's bike,
first time riding a two-wheeler,

his pushes, my breaths, how I pedaled.

Now, passing benches,
an emaciated, bearded man with a hollowed face
lies on one, propped up on full gray trash bags,
hands shaking—

I tell myself not to look.

Think of what Dad would do,
jog back, squish a dollar into the man's cup.

His sign reads:
Homeless, starving, lost everyone.
Lesions on his scalp, his forehead—

like the skeletal men they show in health class,
unprotected sex, flashing at us, warnings.

I scurry away, eyes on the changing leaves,
Belvedere Castle, the pond,
kids chase their mom around the tire swing,
don't look at the trash falling from bins,
don't smell the urine on the rocks,
don't read the SCREW YOU graffiti
sprayed on the old stone wall.
Look at the kids play,
look at the statues,
look up into the blue,
all those buildings framing the sky.

The wind picks up
as I get close to home,
it comes to me suddenly:
The yearbook theme should be New York City.

HIDING

Jimmy, the doorman, says hello,
I push the elevator button, make it glow.

Breath speeding up, can't wait to tell Dad
I've got my theme.

Turn the key.

Walk down the hall.

Go to his room.

But as I turn the handle on his bedroom door—

I hear a yelp.
I hear a *NO!*

And then I see:

James, naked on my parents' bed.

Dad, beet-red, naked,
hiding
his lower body behind the door.

A UNIVERSE AWAY

I drop my backpack. Run.
Don't wait for the elevator.
Chase the stairs down, like a slide.
Run past Jimmy, out onto Riverside.
I make it to the water.
Yell at a boat on the Hudson,
beg it to take me away, under a bridge,
out to the ocean, vast and wide,
beg someone to make me blind,
take me out of this shady city,
to a country, a continent,

a universe away

from here.

BLURRED

My eyes blur,
I don't know what I've just seen.

My legs shake,
the earth has shifted.

THE MILKY WAY

I wander over to Broadway.

All these people

moving in all their directions.

I sit on the bench.
A mom prances with two kids, hand in hand.
Her ponytailed hair straight, a mom
who sings while she vacuums, plans Disney vacations.
Watch them cross.

A man with too many dogs,
barking at him, at each other.

A small concrete island
in the middle of rushing traffic,
a halfway place,
crowds just rush past.

Sitting here
                    surrounded by trash, cars, people,

hanging
in the middle of the Milky Way,
a nebulous mass

containing millions of tiny things
smeared across the sky,

in this crisscross rush,
blinded by lights.

Just one random person
in this ever-spinning city,
never colliding.

Alone on a bench.

Once whole
but now
        I   am
              shattered.

FLOATING

I have change in my pocket,
could use the pay phone,
call Chloe. Dylan.
What would I say?
Hey, what's up,
my dad's gay?

Instead,
I use my change
on the bus

float

back across town.

Run upstairs
to the Yearbook office.

My advisor's there.
Asks if I've thought of a theme yet.

Suddenly New York City feels like a lie.

Fake. Filthy.

I look up at the white ceiling,
dotted with a million pinpricks like stars,
and I say

how about space?

FREEZE-FRAME

Sit at my desk.
Line up supplies
in alphabetical order.
Erasers. Paper clips. Scissors.
Neat in a row.

But I freeze when I get to the stack of layouts.
The Freshman page on top.

April.

I leave the random order,
run back

for her.

THERE ARE NO STARS

Back past Jimmy, the elevator, the door,
not wanting to open it, knowing I have to . . .
How will I look at him. What will I say.

They are there. Huddled in the living room.
Dad, April, Mom. No James in sight. Family meeting.
Whatever that means.

Sit down next to April. Put my arm around her.
They don't ask where I went.
Dad says he's sorry for what I saw,
didn't know I'd be home early.
Mom puts her hand on Dad's knee.
Says she and Dad met in the sixties,
a time of exploration
(like this is a history lesson).

Then she says *we have an open marriage.*
Do we know what that means?

April shrugs. I nod slowly.

It means she knows Dad sleeps with James.
It means they both think it's okay,
     it's something they've agreed to.

It means Mom has lovers too.

Maybe her studio is a place where she makes more than art.

Dad says they've arranged it this way, out of love.

For who?   Not for us.

Dad reaches his hand to me.   Trying to offer comfort.
His fingers look too long,   disfigured.

All of their friends, parties,
the disco lights, red, green, blue, spinning.
Wine glasses. Joints.
April and me. The balcony. Alone.

There are no stars.

Just people   lost   wandering
                                 in the dark.

ABSOLUTE MAGNITUDES

After the meeting, I say nothing to her, to him,
take April, pull her to my room.
She starts to ask me what I saw.
I shake my head, say *let's just play.*
Mancala. All those bright jewels
in all those shallow holes. One. Plunk. Two.

Hear them talking outside the room:
Dad wants to come in,
Mom tells him to give us time.

We do homework.
Help April with hers,
try to do mine.

My Astronomy textbook defines
absolute magnitudes as:
a scale for measuring the actual brightness of a celestial object
without accounting for the distance of that object.

If you get too close,
you might find
the actual brightness of something
can make you go blind.

Sirens go off,
cars on the Henry Hudson never stop,
all those tiny people
in their tiny cars,
driving around their tiny lives.
Brown smog parading
as a night sky.

NOWHERE

If your past is a lie, what happens to your future?

Open my desk drawer,

rip the corners off my Columbia application.

Open my planner,

scratch out Yearbook task lists,

draw blue lines across my hands,

a road map leading nowhere,

decorate page after page
with punctuation.

BEFORE

Before, James was April's Spanish tutor.

Before, James was my dad's Teaching Assistant.

Before, James was the person who played chess with Dad
    for hours.

Before, James was from Michigan.

Before, James had a story for each of his tattoos.

Before, James was fifteen years younger than my father.

Before, James was a drummer for a punk band.

Before, James was the person Chloe thought the hottest.

Before, James would tell me good books to read.

Before, James lived in Greenwich Village.

Before, James was the person who made my dad laugh
    the hardest.

Before, James was my dad's running partner.

He was my dad's best friend.

AFTER

Now

he will never be anything other than this one thing to me:

my dad's lover.

THEN

My dad was:

A teacher,
marked up my English papers, endless lectures on Mesoamerica.

A gourmet cook,
chicken mushroom alfredo, tomato basil salad.

A craftsman,
the one who made his own Halloween costumes.

A movie lover,
the one who took us to see *Back to the Future* and *The Goonies*
      four times each in the theater.

A sentimentalist,
the one who framed every card we made him.

A husband,
someone who stood by his wife no matter where she was.

A parent,
the one who took care of us, woke us up for school on time,
      every day.

NOW

My dad, hidden behind a door, is only this:

another man's lover.

OUT OF ORDER

I.
Dylan calls and says
come to Chloe's.
April at a friend's,
I go, leave a note,
don't ask permission.
My parents don't seem
concerned
with normal
family
rules.

We sneak out,
run down
her fire escape.
Chloe in her Kurt Cobain shirt.
We sing "Come As You Are,"
all the way to Ludlow Street.
Use our old fake IDs,
lie to strangers,
Dylan buys rounds of shots.

Dad and James. The bed.

Shot.

An open marriage. What's always been.

Shot.

Chloe asks why I'm drinking,
I tell her it's Senior year, right?
Time to party.

Dylan gives me weird looks,
but doesn't ask questions.

I try to play the jukebox
songs from when we were young,
"Our Lips Are Sealed," "Love Is a Battlefield,"
but the box keeps flashing red:

out of order.
I kick it once.
Lay my middle finger against the glass.
Dylan laughs, tells the machine it better watch out.
Chloe says we don't need music, just dance,
and so we do.

II.

Next morning, stumble home,
pass April watching *The Wonder Years*.
Worried she will smell me,
I walk fast, manage a small hello.
Mom not here. Again.
Dad waves from the kitchen,

bent over a sandwich,
asks how my sleepover was,
I don't wave
or answer.

Go to my room
but I don't know why I'm there,
reach for my homework,
head pounding.
Can't focus on it,
instead I tear
the Columbia application
all the way
in half.
Why would I want to
follow him there.

Then I go into my closet:
throwing everything
that was once folded—
pink, purple, gray—
onto the floor.

EDGES

Staring up at me
from the mishmash of sweaters
is a piece of the glass fish
I broke when Mom left.
Part of its eye.
Dusty yellow.
Sharp edges.
I sit with it
in my closet.
My stomach sick.
Like hanging on to the ledge of a building,
I squeeze the glass piece
as tight as I can.
When I uncurl my fingers,
red covers the fish's remains,
my palm bleeds
just a little bit.

REARVIEW MIRROR

In an effort to be this so-called family,
we all go see *The Glass Menagerie*.
Mom and Dad think a play about people
more confused than us will make us forget.
In the taxi home, Mom says
they've hired an art therapist
to help us process everything,
some woman named Ann
Mom knows
from the studio.
As Mom speaks, the taxi driver catches
my eye in the rearview mirror.
Pretends he didn't.

I think about the play,
how Laura forgives Jim for breaking the horn
off her tiny glass unicorn,
then gives the hornless unicorn to him,
a symbol of how he
broke her.
I rub my forehead with my cut hand,
catching again the stranger's eyes in the mirror.

Silence strangles all of us, as we fly past

Shakespeare & Company,   H&H Bagels,

veer down West End,
spin the corner,
land right smack on Riverside.

We get out of the cab, Dad never saying a word
about Tom, Laura, the unicorn.
Usually he would've lectured us
on themes, metaphors, symbols.

Now, we're all silent—
evidence left behind
at the scene of a crime,
      lying motionless   on an empty stage.

DREAMING INTO A DREAM

Art therapist Ann, armfuls
of bronze bracelets rattling,

asks us each to draw
a tree,
a house,
a person.

For her, I draw quickly:

trees as streetlights
houses as skyscrapers
people as shadows.

Later, alone:

I take my time, drawing what I want.

Two sisters climbing trees,
gardens to tend, bikes to ride,
neighbors, lawns.
A house, yellow, with a white fence.
A mom, pulling fresh cookies from the oven.
A father, tanned and tall, in a tie.

I hide this drawing under my pillow,
dream myself
into a dream
of a different kind of place,
a different kind of family.

RECORDING SESSION

October

SESSION TWO

(Sighs)
Just going down the line here with these assigned questions.

Three:

How did you choose your career path?

>*I had a teacher in high school who had me tutor other*
>*students. She thought I would make a great teacher*
>*myself. I listened to her.*

Number four: Did you ever doubt your path?

>*Not really. As soon as I got to New York City, I*
>*knew I was in the right place. As big as Texas was, it*
>*doesn't compare. This city's a place where you can be*
>*anyone you want to be. A place where there's always*
>*something to do. Always something new to eat. Always*
>*something happening in the street.*

What does that have to do with teaching?

>*Well, teaching brought me to Columbia, and*
>*Columbia, the city. And the city brought me to your*
>*mother. We met in October, you know.*

Yeah—

> *I'm not sure you know the whole story . . .*
>
> *We were both marching in the Halloween parade. She was a fairy with glass-beaded wings, me a praying mantis. She said, "Nice wings." I told her hers weren't so bad either.*

Dad—

> *We drank wine at a patio bar and watched the parade go by. (Laughs) Both of us had trouble sitting with those wings on, so, after a while, the costumes came off and it was just us. We stayed up all night talking, agreed on so many things . . .*

That's—

> *The value of art and education. The importance of living life with an open mind. Letting love in, never being too rigid about anything—*

Dad!

We're supposed to talk about career here. Not take a trip down memory lane.

> *Well, I was going to say it was that night that your mom inspired me to follow through with my PhD plan and not stop at my Master's.*

(Pause)

So did you finish your application? To Columbia?

I'm not going to Columbia.
I'm not staying in this city.

Oh.

Okay.

That's too bad, I was looking forward—

Number five: What career advice do you have for me?

Play to your strengths. Be true to yourself.

Well, that's funny. Coming from you.

Pardon me?

Be true to yourself? The way you've been true to us?

Miranda—

What if you don't even know who you are?

Miranda. You've always known who you are.

I don't know anything anymore.

NO SPARKLING GOD

Septembers and Octobers we used to find
sequins on the soles of our bare feet,
feathers in the laundry.

Dad and Mom made their own costumes
every year before they met,
and every year after,
except the year she was gone.

They were always closest in the fall,
him poring over her sketches,
her handing him beads, a hot glue gun, a needle,
gifting him splinters of red glass
to glue on his shoes, wands, masks.

The past few years,
Mom and Dad
made costumes of all the
Aztec gods.

This year, they've made nothing.

This year, no one needs a costume.

Masks of Quetzalcoatl, Xochipilli,
big-beaked and feathered,
stare down at me,

line the hallway,
and just like you never really know
what's on the inside of anyone
or any family,
on the outside
they are powerful, beautiful gods.

On the inside they are lifeless:

faces covered with fabric,
bones carved from Styrofoam.

COSTUMES

This year, Halloween night:
April, dressed as an angel,
goes to the parade
with a devil-horned Mom and Dad.
They invite me to come,
even made some wings for me.

I stay uptown, leave my wings at home,
a group of us weave through the Upper West Side.
Bart Simpsons and Madonnas blend in
with the vampires and princesses,
we pass a couple in matching Axl Rose bandanas.

Last year, Adam and I, matching troll dolls,
my hair pink, his orange,
sipped Coke from Solo cups,
R.E.M. blasting from the radio.
We went to the roof,
troll hair blowing up,
he told me he loved me,
loved how alike we were,
his eyes gleaming above me,
surrounded by all those skyscrapers, that navy sky.
I used to think I'd lose my virginity to him.

Now Dylan, in his pirate patch,
calls me Matey, breaks out his flask.
Asks me if I want a sip.

I take two.

Chloe meets us on the street—
a roller-skating candy cane.
Asks what Dad came up with this year
and why I'm not in costume.
I lie, tell her I'm tired, spent all night
helping him sew.
Say my dad's going
as his favorite flower,
one species disguised as another,
a bird-of-paradise.

I follow through the streets,
matching Chloe and Dylan sip for sip,
watch as kids litter
candy wrappers everywhere.

CASSIOPEIA

Yearbook staff's on board
with the outer space idea.

They brainstorm like lightning:
classes in constellations,
faculty in rocket ships,
give each Senior an astronomical mission.

Somehow the theme has given them inspiration—
they draw and choose and pick and label.

As they work,
I feel myself floating
above them,

like Cassiopeia
hanging upside down
in the fall sky.
Try and keep myself focused, occupied,
anything to be away from home.

They ask if I want to see their work,
if I need to check it, I wave my hand, say *it looks okay.*

They ask questions over and over,
I have no answers, I shrug, say *whatever.*

After they've left:

My eyes wander over
their neatly laid piles of layouts,
pause at the one they worked hardest on,
a "field day fun day" collage.

Everyone looks so happy, carefree.
I crumple each corner.

Make a tiny rip through the center,

then keep ripping it to bits.

Eyes.　　　　Hands.　　　　Hair.

Just shreds of people
scattered at my feet.

HOT AND COLD

After school,
I walk right past the unsorted mail.
Dad says we need to talk college—
if I'm serious about not going to Columbia,
then I need to see other schools.
He's trying to pretend things are the way they were,
that I'll be there, hanging on his every word.
I tell him I don't need his help,
I already know where I'm going to apply.
All small schools, away from the city.
He says we should visit one this weekend,
have an informational interview
while there's time.
I sputter a *fine,*
anything to get out of here.

Go to my room.
April knocks,
asks if I'll help her memorize lines
for the school play.

Mom comes in, watches.
April listens eagerly
as Mom offers her advice.
I roll my eyes,
leave them in my room, rehearsing.

I take a shower,
think about spending the weekend
with Dad at some random college,
about Mom helping April,
as if she's always been there
for her,
us.

I make the water icy cold,
then all the way
back to
hot.

IF WE COULD FIND ANY STARS

Sneak out,
Dylan asks if I want to smoke up.
I always say no,
but the way Dylan looks at me tonight,
squinting eyes behind shaggy hair,
his John Lennon glasses on,

I say yes.

We climb the Big Rock
in Riverside Park,

reach the top.

Dylan says I seem different.
I tell him I think he's right,
we're all in Existential crisis.

He says he misses me nagging him about
his college apps, I'll be happy to know
he's thinking of applying early to NYU.

Not long ago, I thought I'd apply early too.
Instead, tomorrow, off to visit some college
in rural Pennsylvania.

I think of telling Dylan about my parents,
how I do feel like a totally different me.
That I don't know what to do with all this change.

Instead, I inhale,
take in the heavy smoke
from the swirly blue pipe.

Breathe in.

Out.
It feels like my head is caught   in a cloud.

Thoughts
        fly away
     as quickly
   as they come.

Dylan opens his
mouth,
it forms a
half crescent
       against the sky.
Goes for another hit.

Exhales loudly,
smoke spiraling from our mouths,
he looks into my eyes,
his pupils full moons.

We lie back

together

on the wet rock,
thoughts shooting in and out.

We would look for stars—

if we could find any.

BREATHE AND SWALLOW

Dad and I,
Saturday to Sunday,
visiting Dickinson College.

Scared to be alone with him
in a car, trapped.
Wish I could
just apply to places, not have to see them,
try to get out of it, say
Chloe needs my help,
there's a Yearbook deadline.
Nothing works.

Dad asks if I want to practice my driving,
I tell him no way.
I haven't gotten behind the wheel
since failing my road test last year.

Turn on my Walkman,
wait for Manhattan to vanish
into the Pennsylvania hills.

Somewhere between here and there Dad asks
if I'm nervous.
A month ago, I would've been.

For a minute
I think about Columbia,
life before,
and something like a lozenge   gets stuck in my throat,
          I try to
                    breathe
swallow
around it.
Wonder how forest and highway
can simultaneously exist,
wind the cords from my headphones
tight to tighter
around my wrists.

GRACE

A brick town square, a flag, a church:
the small town of Carlisle,
the college at its heart,
cradled in farmlands
and Central Pennsylvania hills.

Grace, the Admissions interviewer,
shakes my hand, smiles warmly—

Sitting there,
in this greenhouse of an office,
full of plants and light wood,
I try to put back on my old self.
Talk to Grace enthusiastically
about Astronomy, Yearbook, Peer Mentorship.

She asks about New York City.
Flash to the cyclones of trash,
the homeless, the rush of crowds.

I tell her the city is vibrant, energetic,
but I'm ready for a change,
I need the peace
of small town life, for a while.
I ask her if students can see the stars at night.
And she smiles.

CHANGES IN BRIGHTNESS

I.
On the ride home
watch the trees and hills,
think of Grace and the stars,
wonder if
pushing time forward,
racing past this part
could be just what I need.
If college in the country
will be my bright place,
and I just need to get from here
to there.

II.
Home.
Notice how messy
the house has become.
Laundry unfolded,
dishes left undone.
I pick up a shirt
to fold it,
hear
April and Mom
on the couch, laughing,
throw it back down.
They're eating chips, watching a home video—
the one where April and I made up a play,

Barbies attacked by our Pound Puppies,
enemies first then friends.
They're laughing at one of the songs we made up.
April sings along with the movie.
Dad sits down, right away, to watch,
Mom's hand on his knee.

Video Dad comes in,
so tan and young, with his old friend Manuel.
Sneak a look at Dad, smiling,
I wonder if he's a former lover.
I watch as young Dad touches my head. Young Mira leans
    into him.
Try to remember now how it felt,
being with him,
feeling like the world was safe.

III.

Video Mira is all smiles, bright.
But the star Mira changes in brightness
1,400 times in a year.
Half the time it's visible
to the naked eye,
the other half it can't even be seen
with binoculars.

Standing there,
amidst a family I don't recognize,
I fade, go dim.
Even the flicker of lightness I felt,

the hopeful promise of a new life in the country,
seems to darken.

Sit down,
Dad says.

And April, too, asks me to come watch, please.
Mom pats a spot next to her.

I whisper

no thanks.

Flicker.

Fade

out.

SHREDS

I.

Dad asks if I will make the stuffing
on Thanksgiving.
Usually he does the whole meal without our help.
He says I'm old enough, he trusts me.
I don't want to,
but I do it.

Chop the celery, the onions,
methodically, evenly, like he taught me,
but soon my wrist tires,
the smell of turkey sickens me,
all my pieces go jagged.
When I go to do the bread,
it gets burned, curls up,
blackening the bright red pan.
I touch my finger to the heat, unthinking,
it stings for a minute, then forms
a small white planet bubble.
I don't shred more bread,
don't run my finger under the water,
I just let it all
burn.

II.

We eat, turkey without stuffing,
Mom, Dad, April,

all pretending

nothing is different.

They ask me questions, I say little.

Not knowing what would come out, if I really spoke.

Not wanting to yell at them, in front of April.

Instead, between bites, I squeeze my burnt finger.

At the end of the meal,

I look down to find my napkin shredded,

like torn clouds on my lap.

DEFLATING

Later April and I walk
to Central Park West,
the parade floats, deflating:

Mighty Mouse with shrunken arms,
Olive Oyl's huge foot waves in the sky.

April asks me why did I
burn the stuffing.

I tell her I didn't do it on purpose,
she asks am I sure.

Raggedy Ann falls at the waist.
Kermit dives headfirst.

April says that she likes it better, knowing the truth
about Mom and Dad, that they seem happier now.

Olive Oyl's other foot falls, deflated.

I say *well, you aren't the one who walked in on Dad and James.*
Her face falls. I regret my words.

She says she misses me.
I tell her I'm still here, for her.

We pass people parading home,
hordes of stores sit closed,
streetlights perched like spy cameras,
watching the crowds go,

until April and I are the only ones left
on these abandoned streets.

CHIMES AND CRYSTALS

We're almost back to our street
but I can't go home yet.

On Broadway:
an OPEN sign.

Celestial Treasures.

Dad calls it a woo-woo store, full of New Age junk.

April and I pause,
chimes and crystals rainbow,
tiny unicorns and fairies
freckle purple felt.
I want to reach
through the store window,
sit there, play
with the creatures.
Tell April to be the tallest unicorn,
I will be the fairy who just earned her wings.

Who cares what Dad thinks?

Push open the door,
a shrill woman's voice whinnies
over the sound of bagpipes,

April and I smile at each other,
move further in.

We flip through Goddess Tarot Cards.
Sniff jasmine, sandalwood, eucalyptus.
Spy rows of medicinal herbs, vitamins.
Try on mood rings,
look up our birthdays on charts.

There's a huge star map,
like Mr. Lamb's,
but this one's exploding colors and pictures:
myths that explain the names of constellations.
I read to April,
point out each planet.

But when I turn around,
she's near a woman
with auburn hair
and lilac scarves.
Her name is Gloria,
she can help us,
if we need anything.

April moves toward her,
I pick up a rain stick.

April now
on the other

side of the store,
light as a leaf,
happy she said
with what our family's
become.

I shake the stick

the sound pours over me

like being trapped inside

a waterfall—

April: on one side,
out of reach—

Me: on the other,
enclosed in a pounding curtain of rain.

WINTER

SUMMON A STORM

Harsh winter wind leaves
a cold layer
over everything,
no way to get warm.

Icy air coats
our apartment,
the space between me
and my family.

Insides matching outsides.

At Yearbook, I enter
and they are already working:
the sports pages,
each sport a planet unto itself.
A few months ago
I would've loved to see
this focus, determination.
Now I just want them to go,

spin out, away.

One of them asks where the field day collage went—
the one I destroyed—
I say it's already off to the printer.

A lie that
flies easily from my tongue.

A parachute of lies that
holds me up lately.

They say isn't it early,
I say not for color collages.
They believe me.
I open my desk drawer,
the erasers, staples,
still sit so neatly.

When no one is looking,
I summon a storm:

                    with a thunder
                         I
              hail paper clips   rain tacks

turn order into chaos.

WINTER LIGHT

The office door opens.
Sunlight beams in: Adam.

He says surprise, he's home for winter break.
So relieved I am to see him,
for a second it's like nothing's changed,
my life makes sense and I know who I am.
I run to him.
Hug him.
His smell is something new.

The staff huddles around us, him,
asks what college is like, if he misses Yearbook,
he smiles at me, says he misses other things more.

He's impressed by our layouts,
I shut the messed-up drawer.

Tell him I'm so happy he's here.
He says it is just for tonight;
his family leaves for Jamaica in the morning.

That night, something else new—
we play quarters with his old high school friends.
He says he's been drinking some, college, experimentation.

I nod, tell him likewise, and his friend Dave gives me a drink each time a quarter lands in the Statue of Liberty mug.

Plink. Plink.

Drink.

DEAFENING

Back at his parents' apartment,
I ask Adam if he's been with anyone.
He says none of that matters,
he's here with me.

I tell him just the sight of him
makes things feel calmer.
Easier.

I straddle him on his perfectly made bed.
My hair curtains his face,
his eyes are closed,
and I'm drunk enough not to care
that we're no longer together,
drunk enough to say
one of the things I have to share.
I tell him I wanted to lose my virginity to him
before he left but—

He interrupts me, says
there's no time like the present.
Puts a lock of hair behind my ear.
Traces a heart with his finger on my knee.
My head spins.
I wonder, if I let him in,
if he could light me, even from a distance,

the way the moon is only bright
because it bathes in the sun's light.

Or how sailors look to the North Star
to guide them, give direction.

Maybe Adam could be that for me again.

I look down, up into his eyes.
Nod my head.

And for a minute,
my head buzzing with beer,
all I want is for Adam to
pour himself into me.

His face floats above me,
so close, so familiar,

but all I can see is James, lying naked, on my parents' bed.

And I can't.
I push Adam off.
Tell him no.

He grumbles
geez, Mira, you're going to have to grow up sometime.

I tell him growing up sucks.
He shrugs. Doesn't agree.

The heat clicks on, deafening
Adam's harsh words—

they float out
into

the howling
December winds.

I follow.

WINDSWEPT

Shut the door quietly,

out of Adam's apartment,

walk to the gold-mirrored elevator,

my reflection framed in the warp of its mirror:

just a little girl at night,
on a balcony,
my long knotted hair,
eyes squinting

                      up.

I don't go straight home,

wander a bit in the night,

think about how quickly people can change,

act in ways you don't expect.

An unpredicted storm that
leaves people out,

windswept,

in the cold.

CONSEQUENCES

3am.
I walk past piles of mail,
clutter on the table.
Dad sees my reflection
in the hallway mirror
before I see him.

He tells me to sit down,
says he knows I'm upset,
that I'm trying to punish him
for what happened,
for things being different than they seemed.
He says he never meant for his choices to hurt us.

Somehow this makes it worse,
like he wasn't even thinking of me, April, our family.
I ask him why he's even awake.

He says he's not feeling well,
been up all night, in the bathroom.
Says not to distract him from the issue at hand,
this is unacceptable, I'm grounded—
something I've never been before.
His face changes then,
Dad looks so different
than the person who
used to help me with my homework,
hushed me back to sleep after a nightmare.

This man is
unfamiliar.

But all I say is fine, I'm grounded.
Whatever that means.
He says no going out this week after school.
No talking on the phone either.

He says there have to be consequences
for bad behavior.

Then he walks down the hall,
steadies himself
hand to wall.

In the mirror
I watch
his giant shadow shrink,
disappear.

RECORDING SESSION

December

SESSION THREE

I want to get just a few more questions in before break.

Question six: What would you like your legacy to be? If you could only teach us—or your students—one thing, what would it be?

> *It would be to challenge yourself. Let the world move you. Make something of your own, something new.*

Sounds like a Hallmark card.

> *Miranda—*

Fine. Can you be more specific?

> *Okay, well, this student I had when I was teaching high school Spanish—Camilla. She made her own time travel machine from cardboard when we read* A Wrinkle in Time. *Or the way you and your sister have made videos, written songs, how you feel when you are making Yearbook, how your mom feels when she's making art, or me, making a costume. Just in the zone. Stay true to your art, your passion. I would want you to remember that.*

Why?

> *Because the world can be a confusing, scary place,*
> *Miranda. Not everything will make sense. But*
> *you can control your choices. You can control your*
> *creations. It can help make the world feel manageable.*
> *I see you struggling—*

Question seven: What would you put in a time capsule to
represent your life?

> *(Laughs) That's a ridiculous question.*

Dad. Just answer it.

> *I don't know. A copy of* Don Quixote. *A chess piece. A*
> *feather.*

COLD GROWS COLDER

The week I'm grounded,
time seems to still.
Silent, empty.
I mark time
by problems half-solved.
Paragraphs half-read.

Finally, winter break.
Chloe and I used to spend it having
double sleepovers at my house, playing Clue VCR,
eating cookie dough, shopping on Columbus.

This break,
me, Dylan, Chloe
spend lots of time
getting rocked:

smoking pot on the Big Rock,
listening to Phish at Dylan's house,
the music taking us up,
we laugh so hard I can almost forget who I am.

Sometimes Chloe locks herself in the bathroom,
only lets me in,
I listen to her problems,
then ask her questions
about movies and music.

She says I'm the only one
who knows how to calm her down.

Chloe doesn't know that helping her
with her problems
is the only way to forget my own.

EVERY TRIANGLED SIDE

I.

I bump into James
in the elevator,
haven't seen him since
walking in on him and Dad.
My throat swells.
I can't look at him without remembering him naked.
I look down.

Notice he's bringing up our ornament boxes
from the storage space in the basement.
Four boxes stacked around him.
I don't ask questions, but he explains quickly
that Dad wasn't feeling well again,
Mom had a big project,
Dad asked if he could buy the tree,
bring the boxes up.

I don't offer to help.

II.

Dad lying on the couch,
says what James has already told me.
I tell him I don't need James's help,
Dad says he didn't know if I'd be around.
He sounds hurt, speaks in a voice

that leaves me with no right
to question.

III.

Later, everyone home,
Mom puts on a Christmas CD.
April puts a wreath on her head,
helps James hang the lights.

April seems unfazed by this new "family."
I pretend to look through the boxes.

Blue glass balls that Mom made,
store-bought reds, greens and golds,
a peeled-nosed Rudolph,
a broken-hatted Frosty.

'Tis the season to be jolly!
Bing Crosby croons.

I pull a white unicorn with a red saddle from the box.
The smell of pine drifts
as they turn the tree into a blinking sky.
They all sing "Silent Night,"
I snap off the creature's horn.

Pocket it.

Tell them I still need to buy gifts.

Float out the door.

IV.

On the street,
smoke a red I bummed from Chloe.
Fairy bells jingle as I enter Celestial Treasures.
Dark Side of the Moon on low as a whisper.

I walk over to the crystals:
a shelf of tiny violet cities,
walls of windows,
every triangled side, a light.

I palm one that looks like the skyline.

For a minute I think about getting it for Dad.

Then I remember what I walked out on:
Mom. Dad. April. James.
Together. Playing perfect family.

I go to the earrings,
pick out some star studs, for April.
Gloria is folding tapestries.
Asks me how my sister's doing,
asks with some concern,
I say *fine* (as always).
Wonder why she cares so much.

After I pay, on my way out,
I pull the horn out of my pocket;
bury it in the folds of the window display
before I scurry away.

HUBBLE'S LAW

Adam, back from Jamaica,
left me something in the lobby:
a seashell barrette, a note.

In my room I read:
Sorry for how I acted last time.
Hope to see you next time I'm home.

The shells are so shiny,
like they're still
underwater.

I reread his note.
Feel seasick. Confused.
Not sure what he wants
from me, what I want
from him.

My bedroom phone rings.

Dylan says he's got Phish tickets for New Year's.
In Massachusetts.

Dad and Mom, together, on the couch.
He's reading *I, Claudius,*
she's got her glasses on, tongue on lip,
drawing plans for her new glass animal farm.

I don't ask them if I can go to a concert
or on a trip with friends.
Not wanting a fight, not wanting a no,
just ask if I can go to Chloe's for New Year's.
Mom leans into his shoulder,
Dad nods his head, yes,
okay, I can go.

For a minute they look like the figures from my drawing,
                        perfect, average, normal,
lying, folded, under my pillow.
For a minute, I think about grabbing April,
sitting with them.

But then I remember Hubble's Law:

The closer a galaxy is to us,
the faster it's moving away.

I can't be part of a family
that's built on lies,
they think they can pull me closer,
now that things are out in the open,

but

I've already

drifted
away.

OUT TO SEA

I.

We take Chloe's nonna's Volvo.
Listen to "Sample in a Jar"
fifteen times in a row.
The farther we drive, the more I forget
my parents don't know where I am.
I forget if I even care.

We land on Planet Phish:

> looks like the 1976 yearbook:
> girls in patchwork skirts,
> guys in bell-bottoms,
> hemp necklaces and grilled cheese for sale,
> pot and sweat and patchouli.

We move with the crowd into the indoor arena.

In the hallway,
two girls,
one naked except for overalls,
another in
white-blond dreads,
sell a pink-patched dress
with a pocket gem that shines—
a beaded silver moon.
Immediately my plain clothes feel wrong.

I nod my head to the dress,
shed my jeans and sweater.

II.

During "Run Like an Antelope," we herd through aisles—

bubble gum smoke pours
on us
pink and yellow balloons
rain down
a guy in a ponytail leads me in a wild
do-si-do
swinging me by the arm,
then comes "Auld Lang Syne."
We slow dance.
Ponytail leads me to a corner,
kissing, swimming me into the wall,
his spindly, tattooed arms wrapping me.
I think about Adam for a minute, and who he's kissing.

Ponytail strokes my back,
his cheek scrubbing mine.
He whispers *Happy New Year* in my ear,
fingers my dress strap,
edges his fingers down,
traces the pocket moon.
He asks where I came from,
I think about lying, saying Larchmont or Long Island.
But I tell him the truth.

He says he's heard kids grow up fast
in New York City.

I guess they do.

I pull Ponytail into a darker space
behind the bleachers, let him touch me
where he wants, and I touch him too.
Because that's what New York City kids do.

I float away—
until "Down with Disease" shouts me awake.
My body pulses
in disgrace at this stranger's touch.

I push away Ponytail,
who calls me a tease.

Search for Chloe and Dylan.
My heart beats faster,
my feet quicken
to the frenzy of the music,
building, like gliding under the biggest waves,
water sliding over my back.

When I find my friends,
we dance like we're on fire,
holding hands, jumping waves of flame,

focus on my own breath,
breathe in sweet smoke
fast as fire
slow   as   water.

AS THE CITY LOOMS

Next morning, still in my dress,
smelling of pot, bubble gum smoke
and that gross guy.

On the drive home,
Chloe and Dylan talk
about being Second Semester Seniors,
Chloe sending in her art school application.

My applications still crowd my desk.
I'll do them today, I think. For three schools.
All away from the city.

The highway runs
gray and long—

Dylan yawns, says he's sleepy.
Chloe puts on Nirvana.

Close my eyes too, try not to think of
Ponytail's quick hands.
I dream:

> *We're young. April and I, the carousel.*
> *I'm counting the clown faces that go by,*
> *trying to predict which will come next,*
> *it's hard, their hair keeps changing colors,*

but Daddy's there. He waves each time we pass.
Except for the last time—
it's like we came too quickly
or he forgot.
I see him before he sees me:
his limbs start disappearing,
I yell for him,
but my horse passes by.

When I wake up,
I don't know where I am.
Then everything rushes back in.
Dad, James,
what a marriage means
when it's "open."
How they tried to keep it
closed.
Hidden from us.
The city looms,
I want to grab the wheel,
turn the car, drive the other way,
away from this place,
what I used to call
home.

STORM HALO

I glance at the halo around the sun
before I go in the lobby.
Mr. Lamb said they
can be warnings: storm moving in.
But the sky is otherwise clear.

At the front door,
turn the key,
no one comes to greet me.
Finally:
empty house,
no one to tell me lies,
make pretend.
Head straight
to the bathroom
to wash away
Ponytail's prints.

Open the door—

I am not alone.

I see a figure crouched in the corner
of the shower,
faucet just dripping.

A hunched body
shivering in the water's pool.

Dad.

STARS FALLING

I freeze.
Two thoughts fight to win
a battle in my brain—

    he's naked
    he needs help.

Unfreeze.
Grab a towel.

His body has become so thin.
Ribs sunken in.

Not like the dad I've known.

Dizzy, stars fall in front of my eyes,
he manages a weak *thank you*,
I wrap him in the towel.

Hunching over him,
my feet wet,
I see his skeletal body.

Pause.

A deep breath in,
I pull him up.

BLANKETS

I guide him to bed,
still in his towel,
tuck him under the comforter,
he mumbles *sorry.*
Before I can tell him it's okay,
he's asleep.

I linger for a minute,
standing over his
      thinning hair
      sunken-in ribs
      covered now
      but still there.

TUNNELING

I leave.
Breathe heavy.

    Dad.
    Something's wrong.

Cross the avenues.

I think about the past few months,
    him weak, more tired,
    coughing,
    up all night

    sick.

Pick up speed.
Race across the street.
Down the subway stairs.
Catch the 9 downtown.

Right there in front of me

neon colors:

an advertisement.

Keith Haring cartoons dancing,
telling people to practice safe sex.

I cling to the silver pole.
The train rocks me.

Condoms in the nurse's office now.

Next stop: 72nd Street.

Red ribbons.

I turn from Keith Haring's drawing.

Another train passes.
Slices of other people's faces.

59th Street.

Articles in *People* magazine.
Fathers denying dying sons, rock and rollers falling
from stardom.

Refusing to sit on toilet seats,
take sips from other people's glasses.

Sucked-in cheekbones,
sunken ribs.

42nd Street.

How did he get so thin without me noticing?

34th Street.

The new plague.

More people dying in this city than ever before.

28th Street.

I look around at the car full of people.

Think about infection, how it stirs inside.

23rd Street.

A death sentence.

And I know.

YELLOWED, GRAY

Get off,
take the 9 back uptown.
Home.
April meets me at the door.
Gives me a huge hug, pulls me further in:

Dad's laid out on the couch.
Mom holds his feet, rubs them,
yellowed, gray.

Dad says he's glad I'm back.
That he was worried about me.
He's sorry I had to see him
like that.
He tells us to sit down.

Girls, there's something I need to tell you.

My stomach knots around his words.

He wipes a tear.
I take April's hand.

Try not to cry,
but I know what he's going to say.

I am HIV Positive.

April sobs,
drapes herself across his knees.

I whisper *how long?*
Years he says.

My breath comes quicker.

Mom says they wanted to protect us,
didn't want us to worry,
to take on more responsibility.
He's been okay for a long time.

I can't breathe.

Dad goes on, says he's on new meds,
could still live for many more years.

Mom smiles, says yes, he could,
that they're working on cures all the time.
Says she doesn't have it, James does.

April sobs and sobs.
Mom rubs her back.

Dad says *I'm still your dad, the same man I've always been.*

But whoever this is,

this man

who parades his lover around the house,
who doesn't prepare his children
for what's happening,
who isn't honest until it's too late,
who doesn't realize preparation is protection,
whoever this is,
yellowed, gray,

he is not my father.

NO SIGNS OF STOPPING

Get out of there.

Go.

Mira, where do you think you're going? Mom calls out.

But I just close the door.

Walk the streets, cry.
No destination in mind.
Wish I had my Walkman.
Wish my head would erase itself.
Rewind.

A car runs a red light.

The first time
Dad tried to teach me to drive,
I sideswiped
a STOP sign,
knocked the mirror off the car.

His face grew red when he told me
he wouldn't always be there

to grab the wheel.
Miranda, you need to be careful.

Now I know:
he wasn't just talking about me,
he was talking about himself,
telling me not to be reckless
like him.

And I realize,
every moment until now has masked this truth:
Dad was sick when he helped me with science projects,
essays on *King Lear*,
the *Odyssey.*

Dad was sick when we made eggs benedict,
black-eyed peas, angel hair.

Dad and James fell in love while sickness stirred inside them.

All this time Dad was one thing; I thought he was another.
Things can shift so quickly,
like the flick of a light.

Or maybe they've been changing longer, steadier,
like a sunset,
colors dragging, day left behind,
a long fade into night.

Crossing the avenue,
the light goes yellow.
A warning.
I dare myself.

Run.

CLOUDY GLASS

Hours later,
after wandering the park,
up and down Broadway,
I duck into a phone booth.

The cloudy glass
surrounds me on
three sides.

Through the front pane
I see a little girl with her dad,
holding tight to his hand.
A pang of jealousy nips me.

I fiddle with the quarter in my pocket.
Call Chloe.
She says Nonna called my parents,
told them all about New Year's,
asks where am I anyway,
she's been trying to reach me for hours.
I tell her I went to the movies,
better get home now,
thanks for the warning.

Hang up quick,
keep walking,
home.

TOGETHERNESS

This time when I come in,
April's not waiting at the door.

She's still on the couch,
watching TV, tissues all around.

They sit me down again.
This time, at the dining room table,
by myself.

Mom says how dare I
walk out on our family,
on something
so serious.
I almost laugh in her face:
Were we not serious enough?
Is that why you walked out on us?

Mom says what's done is done,
now is the time
for truth, family togetherness.

She says they know I went to Massachusetts,
they've decided that between that and running away just now,

I'm grounded again.

Suddenly she's a disciplinarian. A real parent.

Dad says he knows I'm upset,
I have a right to be,
but he has lots of time left, don't worry.

As if it's possible not to.

I mumble *sorry*,
ask him how he's feeling.

He says he's been better, but he's okay.
I say that's good,
though I know he's lying.

An awkward silence,
the air hangs heavy,

I head to my room,
leave them there,

her, him

all masks off,
no more lying or hiding
their brand of togetherness,
the signs and marks
of who they really are.

KINDLING

I take that ridiculous drawing
of my dream of a family
out from under my pillow,
rip it to shreds,
like kindling.
I open the window,
throw the pieces into the wind,
tossing my own dream
into the raging
firestorm
of trash.

COUNTING STARS

April knocks,
drags in a bag of Doritos.
Tells me she's scared.
I nod *me too* from my windowseat,
she comes and sits,
we munch chips.
Just like we used to,
we pretend apartment lights are stars.
Count them,
tap the glass with our nails.
Maybe he'll live so long they'll find a cure,
she says.
Maybe we can help,
she says.
I say
How? Find a DeLorean?
Go back in time?

That night April sleeps in my bed,
and for one brief moment,
like the steady light
of this ever-glowing city,
it feels like
nothing has changed.

RECORDING SESSION

January

SESSION FOUR

I'll try to keep this short today. I know you need to rest.

Question eight:

Do you have any advice for me as a Peer Mentor?

> *Teach by example.*

Okay, and question nine:

What's the hardest part of being a mentor?

> *Watching people fail and not being able to help them.*
> *Just like being a parent. Watching your kids make*
> *dangerous choices and not being able to prevent them.*

(Pause)

What about when parents make dangerous choices?

> *Miranda, I know you're scared. We all are. But we will*
> *get through this . . . day by day. All of us, as a family.*
> *Okay?*

Okay.

CRYSTALS DANGLING

Last day, winter break:
April and I, Celestial Treasures,
Dad said I could accompany her,
even though I'm still grounded.
Gloria, behind the glass counter,
huge silver hoops swinging from her ears.
April palms an Animal Spirit book.
I trace Andromeda on the map.

Suddenly, I overhear: April telling Gloria Dad's HIV Positive,
asking if there's anything she has in her store to help him.

I yell her name. Tell her *no*.

But Gloria's already there,
arm around April, tears sparkling, earrings twinkling.

She starts naming funny-sounding pills and herbs:
selenium, St. John's wort, astragalus.

She says this is what they do for their HIV patients
in the Netherlands, India.
Says our dad is one of millions of cases worldwide.
That we need to give him the strength to endure
        these tragic times.
Shows us crystals, talks of Reiki, acupuncture, homeopathy.

Can't listen to
these impossible remedies,
this invasion of privacy.
I leave. Wait for April outside.

Finally, she emerges, bundles of herbs in her arms,
crystals dangling around her neck.

I ask her how she could do this to us,
tell a total stranger something so personal,
so private,
April says *this* is our DeLorean,
this is our chance to save Dad.

She walks quickly home.
I walk twenty feet behind.

STARLESSNESS

That night, I cocoon.

April slides a piece of paper under my door:

Homeopathic medicine is a form of alternative medicine that
uses very small amounts of natural substances, which in larger
quantities would cause disease. The theory behind homeopathic
medicine is that "like cures like," and that a substance that
causes an illness in a healthy person might cure those symptoms
in someone who is ill.

Sounds like a witch's brew.

What's the point of placing hope in that?

Hope as slim
as the sliver of moon
hanging
in this empty,
starless sky.

EXCAVATION

The cluttered dining room table,
a white-blank college essay.
April trots past with her
bottles and crystals.

Dad in the living room with James,
watching a documentary
on an archaeological dig in Mexico.

I return to the essay questions.

Try option one.

How would you describe the defining aspect of your identity?

I type on the blank page:

> *My dad was my mentor. My identity was formed*
> *by watching him.*

April stands in front of the TV,
tells them about herbs, crystals,
Dad and James smile at her, touched.

I delete.
Start over.

James reads a label.
Dad says he's working with the best doctors in the city.

I write:

> *I used to like living in the skies of Manhattan. I identified*
> *myself as a proud New Yorker.*

April gets teary,
says she's not giving up, this could save him,
Gloria has helped others.

Delete again.

They say they'll think about it.
Them.
Like they are their own team.
Their own family.

April leaves everything on the table in front of them.
I turn back to the blank page,
punch the keys hard:

> *Identity is not a fixed thing, but something that evolves*
> *over time. Like an excavation, you never know what you*
> *might uncover about yourself or those around you. What*
> *might change you, forever. Beyond your own control.*

I highlight the paragraph.

Shrink the font,
make it invisible.

As Dad and James turn their eyes back
to the TV,
I shut down my computer,
pick up the keyboard, slam it down,
don't press save.

The archaeologists dust dirt from bones.

WHAT'S ALREADY GRAY

Back to school,
Dad's bought us MetroCards,
a note lying on top of them:
Happy second semester!
I crumple it into a ball,
leave it on the kitchen counter.

April and I fight
the white wind
to 86th Street.
On the bus
she begs me to listen to her.
I say no,
she shouldn't have told,
no, she shouldn't get her hopes up.
I don't say
it'll be worse this way.
If she gets excited about it,
if she hopes for the impossible,
it could crush her.

Dylan slides in next to me,
smelling more like soap than cigs,
humming a Beastie Boys song,
drumming the rhythm on my knee.
He can tell the air's frozen between April and me,
tries to bend it with song.

I don't give in,
there's no way out now.
The snow falls heavier
as we land on Park,
shuffle to the door,
fresh white snow covering
what's already gray.

WINTER DUST

A cloudy first day back,
a useless Peer Mentorship meeting
on peer pressure.
Now, Yearbook.
I'm late.

Some lip-glossed girls say
the advisor was here to pick up
the sports pages, deadline today.
I look at the pile that's half-done—
team pictures, no action shots,
players' names, no font picked.
Picture my old self,
using all I have to fix this.
If only it were that easy.

The staff asks if they can just pick the fonts,
if they can use last year's action pics,
I say *whatever.*

Winter dust coats the white office.
Like the streets and sky, it is graying too.
Who cares about capturing a present
that's almost past?
Stars that look the brightest are
already dead and gone.

PLAYING PRETEND

Mom, Dad, the couch,
a crossword between them,
she gives him his pills,
crystals collect dust,
herbs remain in plastic, unopened.

Later, April sits with Mom,
  each one preparing for her own show—
school play, glass exhibit.
April launches into her herbal plan.
Mom calls Celestial Treasures "darling."

They ask me to join.
Say I'm busy, college apps.
But even if I didn't have essays to write,
even if I wasn't still grounded,
I'd be out with Chloe, at the Big Rock with Dylan.

I wouldn't be playing this game of pretend,
playing family, playing doctor, playing healthy,
as if the world we knew hadn't slipped
  off its axis.

DELETE ALL

Focus in on my essay.
Again.

*Option two: What was a pivotal moment in your life and how did
   it shape you?*

The question screams at me.

I try: *When my mom left us for Italy.*

Highlight it. Turn it red. It seems like a joke compared to

The day I walked in on my dad in bed with his best friend.

Delete.

Try again: *The day I found out my parents have always had an
   open marriage.*

Italicize it.

Then, select it.
Delete.

The day I found out my dad was HIV Positive.

Bold.

A newspaper headline.

Wonder to myself:

Is my dad his disease?
Can protecting someone do more harm than good?
What's the difference between a secret and a lie?

Move the cursor. Select all. Delete.

Instead, I write about scuba diving.

DARKENING SKY

It's barely snowing now
but they say it's coming.

In manila envelopes,
I hold tickets out of here.

Applications to three schools,
Dickinson, Kenyon, Bowdoin,
all the same and all complete,
all in the country, away from here,

away from the gray of New York City,
the city Dad loves to love,
the city I'm ready to leave behind.

I pause
in front of the post office,
packages thick with the
weight of my lies,
experiences I never had,
hoping to earn a spot of peace
far away from here.

As I mail them,
the snow falls heavy,
the sky, darker.

TWO CLOUDS INTERSECTED

Back in the apartment,
empty-handed, jacket wet.

For a minute, excited to tell the old Dad,
I did it, it's done.

I'm greeted by quiet:
see them together
again.

This time
                    out in the open,
                    sleeping

on the living room couch.

James's arm tucked around Dad's back

        cuddling,
                    their heads nestled together
                    like two clouds intersected.

I swallow a cry and like the
                            snow
                             I
fall and melt
                away.

NORTHERN LIGHTS

Later that night,
I spy a new glass bird
perched on the coffee table.
I touch its thin wings,
trace the bright green swirls.
So light, smooth, cool
in my palm.

Mom emerges from the kitchen,
smiling, seeing me holding the bird.
Said she made it
for my future dorm room.
Colored it to look like
the Northern Lights.

I feel myself turn hollow,
holding this flightless bird.

I set it down.
Hard. Make it tremble.

Every day, she makes those animals
so delicately,
purposefully,
every day, adding distance and fractures
to our already broken family.

I ask Mom if she ever gets jealous of
what Dad has with James.

Tears shimmer in her hazel eyes.
But I keep going:
ask her why they even stayed married,
why she and Dad ever had kids.

I don't wait for answers,   just leave her there,
flightless,
with that bird.

BLIZZARD

All night, snow.
Open the window,
stretch my arms out.
Keep my eyes open
in the white, whipping wind.
There are few cars on the highway.
The river's frozen in places.
In a city that never stops,
I can hardly hear anything.

For tonight, the city gives me
what I need.

FLIPPED

Chloe calls,
asks if I'll ever get ungrounded.
I say who knows,
maybe I could sneak out anyway.
She tells me
wait it out, don't make it worse.
Now she's the one with advice.
I hang up.
The world has flipped.

Next, April comes in my room,
says Dad will let me go to the movies,
but only with her.

Asks if I want to hit the closet,
wear funny old coats and hats of Mom's.
I tell her no, grab an umbrella.

At the theater,
nothing's worth seeing,
or the times are all wrong.
Instead, we sip too-cold hot chocolates at Cafe 82,
watch a family eat cheeseburgers,
kids play tic-tac-toe, parents plan spring break.

On the way home,
April says she heard me fighting with Mom.

That she's trying to help him, us.
I tell her I'm not going to pretend
that Mom's been here all along,
when she hasn't.

April stops me,
the freezing rain battling us,
says we can't keep fighting
like this, who knows how much time we have left.
Tells me Gloria says
we need to shine light on our secrets,
it will help us heal.
Before I can say I don't know how,
the wind picks up,
turns my umbrella inside out.

RECORDING SESSION

February

SESSION FIVE

Last three questions. I want to wrap this up today.

> *All right.*

Question ten:

What does empowerment mean to you?

> *(Pause)*
>
> *It means finding your own strength . . . and then using it in ways that make you and the people around you stronger.*

Eleven: How do you approach the unknown?

> *(Coughs)*
>
> *I used to be braver. Now—I'm more—cautious.*

That's ironic.
Twelve: When is it okay to break the rules?

> *When your heart tells you the rules are dysfunctional.*

Bullshit.

Did your heart tell you the rules of marriage are dysfunctional?
Did it tell you to lie to your children?

> *Stop the tape, Miranda.*

No. I've done nothing but listen to you for years. And the whole
time you've been lying to me.

> *Things are more complicated than you realize. Love is*
> *a tricky thing.*

> *Please stop the tape. Take a deep breath.*

No.

> *Miranda, I know you're upset. We all are.*
> *But you can't keep doing this. You can't keep pushing*
> *people away and shutting them out.*

Time's up.

HIS PUNK ROCK FACE

I stop the tape, walk away,
shout that I'm going out.

Footsteps follow me to the door.
Not Dad.
Not Mom.
James comes from around the corner.
His silver eyebrow ring. His blue-black hair.
He tells me he heard our session,
that I've upset Dad.
That I need to let people in. They need me.
I should try to be there more for my family.

My insides burn.

I say

Why do they need me
when you're doing a great job for all of us?

He's not done talking,
but I shut the door in his punk rock face.

THE SPACE BETWEEN

The crosstown bus,
hanging on to the metal bar,
a man with an upside-down newspaper
whistling "My Girl,"
winding through Central Park,
trees heavy with snow,
I wonder
how many people,
like Sam, the homeless man,
are living outside tonight,

what's happened
to the man with AIDS in the park,

if James is telling Dad I walked out on him,
if Dad defends me, or whether he says
something to Mom.

Off the bus, wet toes sting numb
from the walk down Lex,
all the way to Chloe's place.
We sit on the fire escape.

The whole way here
I planned to tell her
everything.

But her eyes look bloodshot.
Hands, wringing.
Tells me she was up too late
with some new guy.
She lights a cigarette, relaxes a bit.
Peering into her leftover mascara-smeared eyes,
it looks like she's
coming apart,
like everything else.
I open my mouth to tell her but
the words stick
to the sides of my throat.

In the space between she whispers
a secret:
Dylan told her that he *likes me* likes me.

I ask her if she's kidding,
ask why she's saying *like*,
as if we're sixth graders.

She slaps my shoulder,
I slap hers back,
send her cig flying,
burying itself—
like all our secrets—
in the old black snow.

WINTER'S GLAZE

In Peer Mentorship,
the theme is bullying.
One girl apologizes to another
for writing "Slut" on her locker
in seventh grade,
another says girls can get away with
bullying because they don't punch,
they just throw words or
give the cold shoulder—

ignore.

My coleader Michael turns to me
like I should have something to say,
some advice to give,
but everything I can think of
is a cliché.
So I pick one,
mutter it.

I tune them out,

look outside,
windows wiped with winter's glaze,
count the floating spots,
till it's all just one big haze.

CHAOS

Later,
the Yearbook advisor finds me in the hallway.
Says we need to talk,
practically drags me to her office.
Says that she knows about the field day collage,
that the rest of the staff met the sports pages deadline,
that they're taking care of all the Senior pages,
she asks me what's going on,
if I care about Yearbook anymore.
My heart aches looking at
the old yearbooks,
the stacks of layout sheets.
But I tell her the truth:
What's the point of celebrating all this
if things can change so quickly—

She says
this is my one warning,
if I don't start showing leadership,
I will be asked to step down from my position.
She leaves me in the room,
alone,
and I toss all the layouts onto the floor.
There's no order in space;

only

chaos.

THOUGHTS ORBIT

I.
Dylan finds me around the corner with Chloe,
hands me something wrapped in newspaper.
Happy Valentine's Day scribbled in Sharpie.
I open it: a joint
and a Phish bootleg from New Year's.

II.
Home,
click in the tape,
remember last Valentine's Day,
Adam took me to J. G. Melon for dinner,
bought me yellow roses.
Wonder if maybe he could be there for me now.
I call Adam and say
    my dad is sick
to a ring that no one answers.

III.
Lock myself in the bathroom,
light a candle,
take two puffs from the joint.
Thoughts orbit
until I settle on one:
Call Dylan,
ask him to cut out early
from school
tomorrow.

BARELY SWERVING

Streets covered in snow.
Dylan says we should ski down the West Side.
The ultimate cutting.
We jet after Astro.

On the bus he says
he feels like something is up with me,
that he's here if I need to talk,
I've always been such a good listener,
he holds my hand.
His fingers are cold and bony.
I tell him I don't want to talk—
just ski.

He says sometimes not talking
is better anyway.
He squeezes my hand again.
Like I'm going to make out with him or something.

We clip our boots into our skis,
use our poles to navigate city blocks.
A station wagon stops short.

I barely swerve around it.

He grabs my elbow, cheeks red
as his winter jacket.
Snow stuck to his hair, peeking out of

his woolly hat.
Tells me I need to be careful.
I tell him actually *he* does,
throw a snowball at his head.

I think about playing tag with him at recess,
how he would always let me win.

For a minute,
I almost tell him the truth.

But the light flicks
from red to green,

I go,
touch his shoulder,
say *you're it*.
We ski down the West Side,
not thinking about the school I'm missing,
Yearbook, my parents, my sister,
just move across the city
as the snow falls

blurring the beige lines
of every

single

standing

building.

SOLAR FLARE

Mom, Dad, the couch,
Dad says the school called.
Where have you been?

I ask him *Why does it matter?*
I'm a Second Semester Senior,
who cares what I do?

He asks what's happened to me.
Who am I?

I say I could ask the same of him.
Mom pats his knee, strokes his hair.
Tells me not to walk away.
I laugh, tell her she's one to talk.

I pass April drawing a sign in her room:
SILENCE = DEATH
it says.

I slam my bedroom door with a flash,

a solar flare

burning on

the surface of the sun.

HOT WATER

Next morning,
James in the kitchen,
white rice in a red pot.
He smells like cigarettes,
black hair sticking up.
I grab a bowl.
Life cereal.
A spoon.
He says I've got a birthday coming up,
asks if I want any rice.
I roll my eyes.
Who eats rice for breakfast?
He says he's making it for Dad.
Mom had to work,
Dad's been up all night,
in the bathroom.

Dad used to hold my hair back
when I was sick.
Now James is up all night with him.

I pour the milk.
Tell James he doesn't need to take care of Dad.
He says he wants to, he loves him too.
I don't give him a chance to say more,

just throw my spoon,
full bowl,
into the sink.

Rice boils over as I leave.

DIZZYING ME

A few days later, swirling down the hallway toward Astronomy,

I hear a sophomore say it:

Her dad's HIV Positive.

> *But how? He's married.*

Are they going to get divorced?

> *Does her mom have it?*

They must be scared.

> *I'd be, like, grossed out.*

> *Did you hear?*

Isn't that awful?

All these questions dizzying me,
but I have one of my own:
How do they know?

My breath comes quick, my head spins,
and I bump clear into Chloe.

CORNERED

She's been crying.
Her turquoise eyes shining.
She pulls me into the corner of the hallway,
asks why I didn't tell her.
My insides shrink,
all I can think to say is I didn't know how.
She asks did I think she couldn't handle it,
that she wouldn't understand or be helpful?
I shake my head no, that's not it.
But I don't say anything
except I'm sorry.
We stand in strained silence,
then the Yearbook advisor
taps me on the shoulder.

WHAT'S FAIR

Chloe knows.
Everyone knows.

April. *April told everyone*
is all I can think
as the advisor guides me
to her office.
Again.

She says I haven't shown I care at all,

I can no longer be yearbook editor.

It's not fair to the rest of the staff,
they can't have someone in charge
who doesn't want to be.

Exhausted, I say *fine*,
walk out.

Punishment only works if you care.

OPPOSITE SIDES OF THE STREET

I bolt out of school,
walk fast to the bus stop
past the diner, the Bagelry.
April calls out to me, close behind,
asks why I didn't wait.
I whip around, say
how dare you,
the whole school knows now,
about our family.

I'm not ashamed
is all she says.

We board the bus,
she keeps talking:
Just because our family is different, doesn't mean it's bad.
I look around at all the people,
all I see is judgment.

I tell April I got kicked off Yearbook.
How Chloe is upset with me
for not telling her first.
Can't imagine what Dylan must think.
April tells me she's sorry but I need to start
letting people in and stop fighting.

I tell her to stop
lecturing me.

We walk home
on opposite sides of the street,
hundreds of people walk past me,
but I've never felt more
alone.

HOLD FAST TO THIS TIME

Sunday morning, a note slipped under my door:

Dearest Miranda,
Happy 18th Birthday!
You're all grown up.
I'm sorry for how hard things have been.
Hold fast to this time,
you only have one Senior Year.
Celebrate!
Love,
Dad

STREETS OF HEAVEN

The night of my birthday,
Chloe invites me to come over
but I say *thanks, no.*
I watch the Oscars, alone.
We used to watch together,
as a family,
place bets.
But April's with James,
volunteering at the Gay Men's Health Crisis.
Mom drawing, Dad asleep.

Flip on the TV.
The red carpet, the gowns.
Who will be the winners:

Leonardo DiCaprio for *What's Eating Gilbert Grape*?
Winona Ryder for *The Age of Innocence*?
Whoopi Goldberg jokes,
Schindler's List wins almost everything.

Tom Hanks wins for *Philadelphia*,
says:
The streets of heaven are too crowded with angels . . .
They number a thousand
for each one of the red ribbons
that we wear here tonight . . .

I make a wish,
push OFF.
The TV flashes once
before it fades to black.

CONSIDERATION

I have never been sent to the principal's office.
Not until today.

My teachers want to talk about my performance in school.
Mr. R says I've shown very little leadership in Peer Mentorship,
the Yearbook advisor says how disappointed she is,
only Mr. Lamb reports
I'm doing well in Astronomy.

The principal says that if I don't shape up,
they will have to take disciplinary action,
that it could jeopardize my college applications.

They also say they know about my situation.
That Mom called them to explain,
told them they should take that into consideration.

They say they're sorry but it's no excuse for my behavior.
I was always so responsible, such a good student, such a joiner.

I tell them I just don't see the point anymore.
I tell them about Hubble's Law:
Things seem close, but really they are far away.

They say I should see the school psychologist,
maybe she can help me.

Get back on track.

Find my way back.

Before I can respond,
the bell rings.

SUPERNOVA

Astro,
I scan the room for watchful eyes.
Take a seat,
Dylan whispers *happy belated birthday,*
asks how I am,
says he's left several messages,
he's heard, he's really sorry.
Tell him I'm fine, try to focus.

Mr. Lamb defines supernovas:

A rare phenomenon
involving the explosion—

The school secretary marches in,

of most of the material in a star,
resulting in an extremely bright—

hands him a note, leaves.

short-lived object that emits
vast amounts of energy—

He reads it.

Mira, come up here.

I can feel all of their stares,
walk quickly to the front.
Could the colleges know how badly I'm doing already?

Mr. Lamb's face floats above
in a cloud of fluorescent light,
he whispers

Mira, your dad's in the emergency room.
Go get your sister, here's your pass.

Then, voice booming:

Class, turn to assignment 5B, and start working.

WHITEOUT

The white of the hospital blasts

as the dark gray elevator opens.

April chews the side of her lip.

I grab her hand.

We march

    down the hallway

       caught in a whiteout

       our only real guide

        vanished.

SKYSCRAPING

We open
the closed door:

Dad, greasy hair,
in a blue-checkered gown.

Tubes cometing outward
from his arms.

James stroking Dad's needled hand,
sobbing,
like this is his darkest white place.

Mom fingers one of her dark curls,
rests her hand on Dad's shoulder.

He looks up at her, nods.
She looks into his eyes,
tells us the HIV has progressed
to full-blown AIDS—
Dad has contracted TB
        and the beginning stages of Kaposi's sarcoma,
which causes lesions.
He has just a few,
nothing internal.

Dad coughs, reaches up to hold Mom's hand,
while James, head down, still strokes the other.

Because of all this, they've given him

one month to live.

The clock hands spin.

The truth tick-tocks:

school, Dad's life,
everything's ending at once.

Dad starts talking but I can't listen:
All this time I knew things were bad
but he still seemed somewhat stable.

I notice Dad's toes peeking out
from beneath the hospital blankets
and for the first time I see
a small lesion on the underside
of his pinky.

I try
to escape,
move the bars off the windows
with my mind—

I jump into the cold

weave through countless buildings

dive into other people's windows

I scrape the sky, scouting for warmer air

fling past rooftops and fly.

SPRING

INDIGO GLASS

A month:
the time it takes
a season to change,
less than half the summer,
the time it takes a baby
to learn day from night.

It's taken less time than that
for my life to
break.

To think of losing him
feels like losing
the ground.

Here, white bottles
of lost hope
filled with herbs
still sit,
gathering dust,
on the indigo glass
coffee table.
I line them now in a row.
Wipe their dust.
Place them one by one in a bag,
head back to the hospital.

A month is enough time
for the moon to fade
and be remade.

But not long enough
to say I'm sorry or
goodbye.

UPSIDE-DOWN KINGDOM

Hover outside the room with this bag of herbs, a spy.
Fight my own impulse to run the other way, fly.

Dad, broken lips, bruised arms, hospital bed.
A rough white washcloth, James pats his head,

reads to him from his favorite book, *Don Quixote*.
I shift in the doorway.

All of spring break spent catching up on homework,
taking turns caring for Dad,
I've been reading him *Alice in Wonderland*,

she almost drowns in a river of her own tears,
lost, confused in an upside-down kingdom,

something he used to read
to us before bed.

James walks out, nods at me,
passes me the rough cloth, a baton,

and, like Alice, given no choice
but to bathe in her own tears,

I take it—
trade places with him,

the cloudy white room of
my own upside-down kingdom,

with cloth,
bag of herbs,
tape recorder
in hand, I wade in.

RECORDING SESSION

SESSION SIX

Dad, I have what I need for school.
But I'd like to keep asking you questions, just because.

> *(Coughs)*

> *Okay, let's keep at it.*

> *What do you have in your sack there?*

The herbs.
Maybe April's right—maybe they could help.

> *(Pause)*

> *(More coughing)*

> *Okay.*

> *(Pause)*

> *I'll think about it.*

(Pause)

Dad, what would you like to do ... with your time?

> *Finish reading* The Byzantine Empire. *Cook. Create. Spend time with the people I love.*

(Pause)

Dad, I'm sorry for—

> *I know, Miranda. It's okay. Me too ...*

> *(Coughs)*

> *Could you pass me a tissue?*

Sure.

> *(Coughs)*

> *Mira, you, you have to—*

> *(Coughs)*

> *make a future you are proud of—*

Dad.

> *Life's short, Miranda. Make it matter.*

Okay.

I know.

(Pause)

I will.

LIT BRIGHT

FULL MOON, 24 DAYS LEFT

i don't take a cab
the end of March air coats me
it is cool breezy and my jacket is thin
but after the hospital i just want to walk and
savor time the moon is full follow it down
the city streets one month and almost a week's
passed already Dad's words about my future en-
circle me i know i need to use the time left
to grow love from something waning
to something waxing, watered,
bright, round, full

ANOTHER LAYER

Dad home in a few days,
I sit and do homework.
Time seems to slow
if you focus on words, facts, solving problems.

Interrupted by April, crying.

I rub her back, tell her
I brought him all the bottles.

Told him I think he should take them.

She smiles through tears,
goes out to see Gloria.

Mom's doing laundry, sorting, folding.
Guess we all have our ways of coping.

Wander into the kitchen, wonder what Dad
would cook if he were home.

Pull ingredients: Onions. Tomatoes. Noodles.
Dice onions evenly. Measure. Pour.

Brown the meat. Pink fades,
a nest of oil fills the pan.

Move the cheese along the grater,
Mom walks in.

She asks how Dad was today,
if I'm ready for school tomorrow.

I say he seemed okay, ignore the school question.
Keep grating.

She says she wants to answer the question I asked
months ago:
why she had children.

I pause.
Keep my head down. Continue.
Chop tomatoes, pieces pool in juice,
seeds swim and scatter.

She says she wanted to do things differently than her own mom,
says she fell in love with Dad fast,
wanted him, only him, to be the father of her children.

She says wanting children is different than having them.

I stir the onions in with the tomatoes.

We scared her. Our need. He was better with us, always.

First layer into the pan. Neatly laid.
Noodles, meat, tomatoes, cheese.

I know I've made mistakes, missed a lot, but
I'd like to be your mother now, if you'll let me,
she says, touching my shoulder.

I shift slightly under the weight of her hand, swallow down
the lump in my throat,

don't say anything, just cook—

she watches, stays by my side,

I add another layer to the clear glass pan.

SIXTY MINUTES

Lasagna's perfectly done—
crisp along the edges,
soft center,
but Dad's not here to eat it.

April's still out with Gloria.
Mom and I sit at the table,
silent, paralyzed.

We leave the lasagna untouched.
Move to the TV.

60 Minutes is on.
Giuliani speaks about cleaning up
the crime in the city,
about *the power of individual responsibility,*
then a story
on the National Institutes of Health
funding new grants for AIDS research.

Mom murmurs *about time.*

They say with new money
they will have a better chance of
finding a cure.

Mom making an effort,
Dad considering the herbs,
April's hopeful eyes—

I look into the Sunday night sky—

lights blink, planes glide
above boats slowly floating upriver
alongside cars zooming fast, uptown and down,
next to a park holding people—

time moves past me,

so many lives

suspended

inside this one moment,

my heart beating fast, breath shallow,

I can hardly feel

the difference between hope

and fear.

A REVERSE CRYSTAL BALL

First day back,
April and I march in,
locked arms.

Quick hugs from Dylan, Chloe.
They ask me what happened, is everything okay,
I say not really,
I'll tell them more after school.
I focus on my classes.

After school, surprise:
Adam's there.
I find Chloe and Dylan,
tell them I'll catch up with them tomorrow.
They give me a look,
turn, leave.

Guilt flickers,
but Adam's smiling big at me,
holding a container of ice cream.

Looking at him's like looking into the past.
A reverse crystal ball.

For a minute,
so easy to forget

everything that's happened.

Adam used to be something solid,
maybe if I let him,
he can be that for me again.

He whispers in my ear
how much he missed me,
he brought me mint chocolate chip—
my favorite.

Ask him why he's here.
He says he has some exams,
studies better at home.
Says he felt bad
he missed my birthday,
asks what I did to celebrate.

I mumble *nothing really* as
he hands me the ice cream.
I cup it till
it frosts
my already chilled hands.

SQUINTING UP

We sit on the steps
of the Museum of Natural History,
eating ice cream in the cold.
A spring day that feels like winter.

A toddler runs up the stairs,
his mother carries a stroller.
Her eyes squint up
like they might catch him.
A guy with a plaid ski hat
sells pretzels from a street cart.
Taxis speed down the avenue.
A bit of early moon, purpling the sky.
The moon's still a crescent,
soon it will be new.

Adam asks if I want to go to the gem room,
teasing me, we kissed there once,
he said I had lapis eyes.
I start to tell him
things have been really hard.
I want to talk
but—

He stops me then, kisses me,
takes a second too long for our lips to align.
Says
he's sorry,

he has felt bad
about that winter night.

Says
he wants another chance,
he'll be home for the summer.

I pull away.
But I can't find the words for:

> My broken family.
> My dying father.

Can't find a way to tell Adam that:

> I almost destroyed the yearbook.
> They kicked me out.

His knee shakes,
eyes flit to a girl
across the street.

Instead of any of those truths,
I say the only thing that wants to come—

Ask Adam if he'll be my date to prom.

He kisses me again, harder, rough,
presses my back into the steps,
says yes.

TO FIND THE SKY

That evening, I go to Adam's.
Mom says okay even though it's a school night.
Feathered sunset clouds float me down
the city streets.

Says his parents are gone,
leads me to his room.

He used to be my North Star.
Always there,
giving direction.
Lighting me up.

Now when he kisses me
it feels all wrong.

I tell him
we need to talk,
I've been keeping something from him.

He nods.
I tell him
I'm no longer editor
of the yearbook.

His brow folds in confusion,
considering my words.

I tell him how stressful Senior year has been.
It was too much,
I had to let something go.

He says that doesn't sound like the Mira he knows.

I nod my head,
tell him I've changed a bit.
One truth at a time.

Then he smiles at me,
says he's glad I told him.
Says he feels like he's changed too.
College is harder than he thought it would be.

We lie down together.
Eyes locked.

Our bodies move together.

This time, I'm ready.

Adam slides the condom on,

says he loves me.

A siren wails outside.

A phone rings.

I breathe in his Tide sheets.

Stretch my neck to find

the sky,

those feather clouds.

Look into his eyes, my past,

let him sink

all the way in.

SO MUCH LIGHTER

Sex hurt just a little
but it was also so short,
hard to imagine
why I waited so long
for something that
felt so much lighter
than the weight
it carries.

INNER-DISTANCE

Staring now
into Adam's eyes,
I know this is it.
As close as we are now,
there's an inner-distance
where my truth should fit.

My naked body curls into his.
His arms big, circling me.

I tell him I wasn't
being completely honest before.

He says okay,
uneasily.

I tell him:
I got kicked out of Yearbook.
Stopped doing my job,
my world
        turned upside down,
what was important before
didn't seem that way
        anymore.

I tell him:
My dad has AIDS. He's dying.

He moves his arm out
from underneath me.

Asks if he had a transfusion
or something.

I tell him no—
my parents have an open marriage.
They both have lovers, men, women.

He asks
what the hell is an open marriage,
stands up, backs away,
says isn't that a contradiction in terms.

I cover myself with a sheet.

He puts his underwear on.

Says that's crazy.
A sprinkle of his spit lands on my cheek.

I wipe it away.

Look at myself in his spotless mirror,
cheeks flushed, hair messy.

He says:

I can't believe you kept this from me.

All this time, and—

I can't trust you, Mira.

Asks how I could let us be intimate, without telling him.
I say I don't have it,
he doesn't have to be scared.

He says he's not scared.

He's disgusted.

That AIDS is a deserved disease.

Something people bring on themselves.

I get up,
dress quickly.
Ask how dare he say that about my dad.
He tells me I should get out of his room.
Tells me I can forget about prom.
I can forget about him.

I can still feel him inside of me
as he pulls his sheets off his bed.

I tell him I'm sorry
for hiding the truth,
but it wasn't like he'd been there for me.
And he doesn't have to be so nasty.

I'm still me.
He asks me how dare I say that,
I'm the one who betrayed him,
whoever I am
is someone he doesn't recognize.

CRASH

I don't wait for the elevator,
I fly down flights of stairs,
almost crash into Adam's parents in the lobby.
Adam's mother,
caramel bob,
coral nails,
his dad in a suit.
They kiss me on the cheek,
tell me they hope to see more of me.
I kiss them back blindly,
thunder booms outside.

Feather clouds swallowed
by a crashing, storming sky.

STRANDED

The
North
Star
may
be
constant
but
it
is
still
four
hundred
and
thirty
light
years
away
from
those
floating
lost
and
stranded
here
on
Earth.

DRENCHED

I walk the blocks,
rain drenching my hair, my clothes
down to my underwear,
I think I remember
knowing this boy,
that he was someone
who made me feel safe.
That he was someone
I so often agreed with.
Now he is someone
who has shamed me.
Shamed my family.

I walk the streets,
trying to remember,
block by block,
drop by drop,
who I am.

SOAKING

Soaking wet, I arrive home.
Mom asks if I'm okay,
I lie, say *yes, thanks,*
pour myself into a hot bath.
Scrub until I can no longer
feel
Adam's touch
or
words.

OUT MY WINDOW

Next day, wake up,
don't want to waste energy, time
on Adam, who obviously
doesn't love, respect me.

Doesn't know anything about my father.

I will Adam's words to
float out of me,
out my window,
sink all the way down
to the bottom
of the Hudson.

Where they belong.

WHAT WE ARE MADE OF

Before school, Mom takes us to get TB tests
to make sure we didn't catch it
from breathing in Dad, orbiting his space.
The doctor gives us a sheet, what to watch for,
what could grow.
I wonder how scared Dad was when he had his HIV test,
long ago.
Wonder who went with him. Mom. James.
Or if he went alone.

April and I clutch hands,
hold each other up as we
breathe deep,
lock arms,
march in.

I enter Astro late,
Mr. Lamb's talking about Carl Sagan.
A quote of his on the board, underlined:
We are made of star stuff.

Mr. Lamb goes on to say, whether or not any of us believe
in something spiritual, we are connected,
we all share matter.

I slide in next to Dylan.
Write him a note:
Is this astronomy or philosophy?
He writes *same thing,*
asks how I've been.

Look down at my injection site, so far nothing's grown.
Shrug, not sure what to say. Thoughts of Adam come too close.
Look at Dylan, push them away.

Write a note to Chloe,
an apology for ditching her for Adam.

Draw Dylan a doodle of a girl,
me,
floating above it all,

head shaped like a star.
He takes my pen,

transforms my star   into a heart.

A BOMBARDMENT

Spot Chloe down the hall,
walk toward her,
            note in hand
            pass it over
till the school psychologist
gets in my face.

Blocks my path.

A bombardment.

You're spending your free period with me,
she commands,

drags me to her room,

down a tunnel, second floor.

Says Mom called,
told her how sick Dad is.

I fold one hand into another,
don't look at her.

In my head
I curl up into a ball.

Spin fast through the sky.

Feel the wind in my eyes.

Focus on the veins in my hands.
Intersecting highways.
Wish I could ride them
away from here.

She asks if I'm listening.

I nod, find a split end. Pick it.

Her volume increases,
tells me she can't force me to talk about it.
But she knows, from experience, that being honest
and open with people, no matter what you're feeling,
can make a difference. Make things better.

I don't say anything—

wasn't I honest, open with Adam?
That made things worse.
I focus on my fingernails now,
how fast they keep growing.
Can't stop time from changing anything,
bit by bit, cell by cell.

Can't stop time from flying.

She finally lets me go, a last plea,

that she's here
if I need her.

Before I go,
think of Dad,
will myself
to stop and
look up
into her eyes,

surprised

to find some kindness

floating in them.

I
take a deep breath and
ask—

tears unexpectedly forming
in the corners of my eyes—

if when I'm gone

she'll be here

something   suspended, strong

able to help
my sister.

WHAT THEY THINK

I.
Almost two days since the test,
three since Adam freaked out on me,
and since I lost my virginity.
At least none of us have shown any sign of TB,
wonder what James's skin would show,
wonder if he's sick.

After school,
we sit in the waiting room,
the nurse wheels Dad
down the hall.

Tall, blond,
all cheekbones,
clothes hang off him.
Two lesions on his forehead.

A disease that hides,
then eats people alive.

We follow behind,
past a child with a broken leg,
a pregnant woman breathing loudly.

II.

Outside.
Several empty cabs pass us by.
Do they see the lesions? Are they scared?

One stops.
I wonder,

does the driver care that Dad's here,
breathing, in his space?

III.

We struggle into the lobby,
James holding up one side of Dad,
Mom, the other.
We share the elevator
with the woman from 14B.
She doesn't look at Dad.
Doesn't look at his lesions
or his skinny, bruised arms,
the way he cannot hold himself up.
She ignores all of us.

Finally, home.

Dad looks at his nightstand,
scattered with crystals—
blinking hopes of healing—
his own shelf of tiny purple cities.

Says okay, he'll try the herbs.

Relief and fear
pulse through my veins.
April smiles wide.

Mom tells us nice work, they're beautiful,
fetches Dad tissues for his coughing,
James rests in the reading chair,
Dad lays down to sleep.

HOW MUCH TIME

WANING GIBBOUS MOON, 20 DAYS LEFT

Next day, in the cafeteria,
pick at a bagel, Chloe and Dylan
at the diner together.
I would've gone too
if I could find the courage to tell them:
My dad is really sick.
He has less than
three weeks left.

I take deep breaths,
eat small bites,
don't think about how much time I've wasted
hurting rather than helping.

After school, after Peer Mentorship,
Gloria's coming.
After school, a plan.
Focus in on Dad,
while there's time.

CONSUMING

Dad, head in Mom's lap,
her reading *The Byzantine Empire* aloud.
She's got tissues, water glass, pill.

April and Gloria come in together,
we all gather round.

Gloria says TB
used to be called consumption,
it consumed from within.
Says we need to strengthen the body,
the lungs specifically,
thank goodness, she says,
Dad doesn't have pneumonia too.
She says he needs more vitamin D
to help slow the progression of KS,
acupuncture can help with that too.

I take notes as she speaks.
She pulls out more bottles:
Astragalus. Mint. Green tea.
Then: bananas, oranges, pineapple juice.

Dad raises his eyebrows,
we catch a smile between us,
a New Age Mary Poppins,
Gloria with her big black bag of remedies.

She asks if we've ever
heard of custard apple,
breaks open a green pale bumpy fruit
with her hands.
Tells April to fetch a spoon for Dad.

As he tries this strange fruit, the herbs, the juice,

I wonder if we can stop time from consuming him,

consuming us.

I wonder if we try hard enough,

we can stop time

from   flying.

THE HOURGLASS

Days march on
grains mount
pills swallowed
breathe in
out
tick
tock
try to slow
the falling
sands.

BLUESHIFT

Mr. Lamb says a blueshift means
that an object is moving toward
the observer.
The larger the blueshift,
the faster the object is moving.

Time is only speeding up.

The principal and I have
a disciplinary check-in.
When I get there, it isn't just her—
Mom's there
in a dark blue suit,
pen and notepad ready,
like she's auditioning
for the role of a sitcom mom.

The principal says
according to teachers
I've been coming to class,
turning in homework,
I seem to be back on track.

Mom apologizes for my past behavior,
says that this year's been stressful,
that Dad's been given very little time.

I tell the principal that she doesn't have to worry,
that I know life is precious,
I want a future I can be proud of.

The principal shakes my hand,
says she's glad to have me back,
hopes my dad gets stronger soon.
I look at Mom, who smirks a little,
both of us wondering what part of
very little time
the principal doesn't understand.

Mom, in blue, comes closer still
like she wants to hug me goodbye.
I let her touch my shoulder,
wonder if someday soon
I'll feel like moving closer.

BECAUSE THE PEOPLE
INSIDE IT ARE

That night Mom, still in her suit,
asks if she can come in,
sits on my bed.
I shrug. Turn a bit in my windowseat.
She says she wants to tell me something:

She didn't only go to Italy for work,

she left because Dad fell so hard for James,

she didn't know how to exist
on the periphery of their love.

She says Italy was amazing, she learned
more during that year abroad than she had in her
whole life as an artist. But when she got
that call from Dad

she gave it all up.

I came home when he got sick.
I came home because he needed me.

Then I knew, someday, we'd be sitting here.
Counting time.

I look at her.

I came back to be with you.
To be with your sister.
As a family.

She says she's sorry for how much she missed that year.

And all the other times she hasn't been around.

I ask her if April knows the truth,
she says she will talk to her too.

I used to imagine she saw us as a train
she could ride at will,
instead of a station,
fixed, every day.

I wonder now if maybe
a family is neither of those things
but something stable,
yet always changing,
because the people inside it are.

I move from the windowseat.
Don't hug her or thank her,
but I do ask her
where on earth
she found that suit.

She laughs.

After she leaves,
I find the buried broken fish
in the bottom of my closet—

carry the pieces to the bathroom sink,

wash them one by one,

lay them gently
to dry
on the ledge.

CONNECT FOUR

Last Quarter Moon, 18 Days Left

Dylan calls,
he misses me,
can he come over.
So little time left
before school is over.
I take a breath,
say okay.

When he arrives,
I try to walk him straight to my room

but he stops—
looks around—

touches every piece of art:
Dad's masks,
Mom's glass creatures,
says my parents are
sort of geniuses.

Dad calls out, asks who's here,
tells us to come say hi.

I pause.
Dylan smiles at me
sideways.

We plunk down the two steps to the living room.
James there too.
For now,
another day,
another round of chess.

Dylan says
he likes James's Alice in Chains shirt,
Dad asks Dylan about college.
I watch Dylan's eyes
scan Dad's hollowed face,
his hair sticking up,
small lesion scabbing his mouth.

Steer Dylan to my room,
we pull out Connect Four.
I'm red. Dylan's black.
About to put my first piece in—

he blocks my hand, holds it,

says *Mira, I'm so sorry.*
Why didn't you tell us?
I say *I didn't know how.*

Then I say to myself, as much as to Dylan:

The HIV's progressed to full-blown AIDS.
He's dying.

Tears in his eyes,
Dylan says *I know,*
he has a cousin
who has it too.
I tell him I'm sorry.

Suck in my breath.
Tell him my parents
have an open marriage.
He nods.
Tell him Adam
thinks it's all disgusting.
Dylan says
Adam's a jackass.

We play the game,
drop
pieces in.

As the chips fall and land,

truth fills the space between us,

and, one by one,

red over black under red,

my heart lifts a little,

we both win.

SPRING WIND

Need to find Chloe,
need to tell her the truth.

But the school lobby's mobbed,
kids crying, hugging—
Chloe at their nucleus,
crying the hardest.

Dylan next to her, pale, dark-circled eyes.
I ask him what's going on.
He says Kurt Cobain's dead.

Chloe reaches for me.
Pours into my arms.
Walks with her head
bent on my shoulder.

Spring wind goosebumps our arms,
sun peeks out from behind buildings.

I lead her to a stoop.
She says she can't believe
he's dead, through
gasping breaths.
She was obsessed with him.

I'm tempted to hide my truth again,
focus on Chloe's pain,

so sad about this rock star
she's never met.

But I can't—

Chloe, I need to tell you something,
grab her hand.
My dad's HIV has turned into full-blown AIDS.
He was given a month to live.
Today is day 15.

She stops crying right away.
Wipes tears with the back of her hand.

She says
oh my god, I'm so sorry.
Holds me in a hug.

I tell her I'm sorry
for keeping everything from her.
I didn't know
how else to deal.
I also tell her about Adam.
How hateful he was
just after
I lost my virginity to him.
I ask her if she thinks I'm a liar.
She doesn't answer,
just says:
she loves me
for who I am.

SPROUTS FROM SKELETON TREES

At home, Dad's eyes bright,
he's in the kitchen,
warming soup.
I tell him about Kurt Cobain,
he shakes his head, sits.

Mom and April, in the living room,
practicing lines for the spring play.

Feeling lighter,
after confessing everything
to Dylan, Chloe.

I stick my head out the window,
a breath before I start my homework.

Even though it's chilly,
faces of green leaves poke out,
sprouts from skeleton trees.

PINK WAKE

Dylan, April and I walk through the park,
the sun, full and pink,
they chatter about the AIDS Walk,
how they can't wait to be part of it,
my heart sinks a little,
thinking about May.
How can they look forward
to walking with other people
when Dad might not be alive?
Would he even want us to walk?
Show our pride?
Is *he* proud?

When April and I come through the door,
Dad's smile couldn't be bigger—
his face looks almost round.
Three envelopes in his hands:
Kenyon, Bowdoin, Dickinson.
We tear them open together,
like kids at a birthday party.

Everything else fades away
Dad beams

the sun sets
leaving a wake of bright pink
in the silvery spring sky.

BUT, FOR A WHILE

We toast
      me
      Dad
      April
      Mom
with Geneva cookies,
ginger ale,
custard apple.
Celebrate my acceptances to
Kenyon
Dickinson
(wait-listed at Bowdoin).

A year ago
I would've been devastated by a wait list,
but not now,
only joy.
Grace even put in a note,
she saw a meteor shower,
hopes I choose Dickinson.

We celebrate with a game,
the four of us, a family.

Chinese checkers:

April's green.
Mom, red.
I choose blue.
Dad, white.
The board, a star.

None of us say much during the game,

marching pieces from our individual sides,

but for a while

we are all jumbled up,

jumping over each other to get to new spots,

until we settle back in
                    rearranged   but   connected.

EXOPLANET

It's been a month and a half since
I was kicked out of Yearbook.
I still have a key but
it doesn't feel like my space
anymore.

Knock on the door,
ask the advisor
if I can talk to her
in the hall.
She says they're trying to make their last deadline,
which is tomorrow.

Deep breath,
tick,
exhale,
tock.

Mr. Lamb says
there are exoplanets that orbit
stars in systems they are not a part of.
Force their way in.

I say I'm sorry
I couldn't be
the leader I wanted to be,
the leader she hoped I would be.

Say I'd like to help now,
if I can.

She tells me it isn't her
I need to apologize to—
lets me past her
into the room.

I apologize to the staff,
tell them I cut up
their field day collage,
almost ruined the yearbook.
I thank them for doing my work for me.
Ask if I can help today,
their last day.

They all look at each other,
look at me.
Ask why I stopped caring,
say they respected me.
I tell them I've been having problems at home,
maybe they've heard.
Tell them I would really like to contribute.

They pull out a layout sheet,
let me in.
The last of the Senior pages—
I draw boxes,
label photos.

Easy
but it feels good,
I do it quickly,
the ruler
cool and smooth,
something solid
beneath my thumb.

LIKE LIGHTNING

Saturday,
April and James volunteering at the GMHC.
Mom at the studio.
It's just me and Dad.
His energy's high,
laughs like lightning,
almost like a hyper child,
just me taking care of him.
Hand him his daily herbs and pineapple juice,
he makes a face but gulps them down.
I ask him if he's up
for a drive.

RAIN ON THE DASH

Slide into the driver's seat,
hands at 10 and 2.

Adam tried to teach me,
Dad too.
But the rushing traffic,
joggers with strollers,
weaving bikers,
learning to drive in the busiest city in the world?
No thanks.

Here we are,
back again,
me shaking
behind the wheel of a car.
Turn the key slowly.
Dad in the seat next to me.

I put on the blinker,
pull out into the street.

It starts to drizzle,
raindrops fall slowly
into each other,
taking their time.
Others run quick.

Dad says learning to drive
in inclement weather is essential.

Focus my whole self on the road.
For him, for me.

This time it's not as scary as I remembered.
I glide up 96th Street.
Roll back down to 79th.
Do one exit on the highway.

Though my right turns are a bit wide,
my braking a bit slow,
Dad says much improved, good job,
we'll do it again soon.
I hear his voice catch,
soften,
wobble,
like a drop sliding down the dash.
My view now obstructed by more than just the rain.

RECORDING SESSION

April

SESSION SEVEN

Okay, Dad, I want to ask you some more general questions about all of us.

What do you love about April?

> Her playfulness. Her openness.
> Her courage and passion, her soulfulness.
>
> But I worry about her too. Sometimes she feels things really strongly.

Makes her a great actress.

> It does.

I worry about her too.

(Pause)

Dad—why did you marry Mom?

> *(Coughs)*
>
> I fell in love with her while watching her work.

Your mom—she has an eye for beauty like no one else
I know. A desire to show it to the world.

So you admire her?

    I do—of course.
    I hope, one day, you will see what I see.

    And you know what I love about you, Mira?

No.

    Your insightfulness, your perception,
    how deeply, and sensitively, you take in the world.

Yeah?

    When you were little
    you would watch the kids play at the playground
    for a while before you joined in.
    You didn't just rush right in,
    but you didn't stand watching forever either.
    You did it your own way. When you were comfortable.
    I always thought that was smart.

Thanks, Dad.

    And there's another thing that I love.

What's that?

That you've made these.

The recordings?

Yes. That way I can always be with you.

WISHING STAR

When we were little
April and I used to climb
Dad's huge body. He would say
girls, I'm not a piece of furniture,
laugh anyway.

Now acupuncture needles slight as whiskers
climb over his wide forehead,
his naked calves,
dry hands.

Mom asks how it feels and he says
some are a quick sting, just a mosquito bite,
others like opening a gaping hole.

Gloria says every time his tummy grumbles,
it means his Chi's moving, it's a good sign.

With each grumble,
each dancing needle,
I dare myself to
hope
like a child,
hands crossed
at her windowsill,
eyes locked
on a wishing star.

GLUE, SCISSORS, TAPE

April, in her room,
newspapers, magazines,
glue, scissors, tape
          at her side.

I ask her what she's making,
she looks up,
says she's making a collage for the Walk.
She's trying to get more people involved.
Says I should come to the meetings.
I tell her I'm not so into hanging with James in my spare time.
She shrugs, says she might join ACT UP
next year, a group that's more hard-core than GMHC.

          Cut
          cut
          glue.

Says *Mira, they're so thin.*
Whoever they are.
Africans.
Children who had blood transfusions.
Men, like Dad.

I tell her she needs a break,
pull her up,
look down
at all the photos,

so many people,
different colors
ages
races,
but all with the very same
face.

TWO CITY GIRLS

We hit the closet on our way out,
cloak ourselves in Mom's jackets, big shoulder pads,
April in cheetah print,
me in shiny coral,
grab umbrellas, huge purses.

See *Four Weddings and a Funeral*,
expecting more laughs than tears,
eat peanut M&M's,
popcorn,
drink Cherry Cokes.
We laugh until we cry
and my heart gets that stony feeling—

not knowing the death would be from AIDS.

On the walk home,
April says even if Dad lives
longer than we thought,
I'll still be leaving.

Guilt rolls in
thick like fog.

I swallow hard,
keep in my cry,
point to purple and yellow crocuses,

poking their heads out around a
concrete-imprisoned tree.

I tell her not to worry,
she can come visit me—
and I tell her a story of

two city girls picking flowers under a starry country sky.

COUNTING TIME

Waxing Crescent Moon, 7 Days Left

Friends chant in the hallway:
count down the days,
the hours,
till prom,
graduation.

My clock counts time by T cells,
which seem to be holding for now:
dancing needles,
crystals around his neck,
the smell of sage hanging
in the apartment air.
I count time by platelets
and Dad is at 5,000—
only one-thirtieth the amount
of a healthy person.

Do I dare

at 5,000 platelets

     with no date

pick out a dress?

Do I dare

look to the future?

rush across the sun?

gallop past the moon?

OPEN STAR CLUSTERS

FIRST QUARTER MOON, 2 DAYS LEFT

My Astronomy textbook says
open clusters of stars
are easier to study
than isolated stars
because they are almost
the same age
and have almost the same
chemical composition.

Scientists
get to know stars better
when they live in these clusters
than when they live

out
isolated

    alone.

Then they are hard to study,
hard to tell
when they fade or glow.

I come out of my room,
to find April.

She's drawing flyers for the AIDS Walk.
I sit down with her, ask her, please, if I can help.
She says *sure,* hands me white paper and a black pen.

I write in
black
bold:
FIGHT AIDS. WALK TALL.
Line my poster with
clusters of stars.

MORNING STAR

Waxing Gibbous Moon

day
0
wake up
hardly slept, my palms scattered with crescent
marks from my nails dug in, he's
awake, alive, i grin and
kiss him on his
cheek on the way
to school   april
and i   walk
hopeful   together.

SIP SWEET SIPS

Come straight home after school,
Dad's showered and dressed.
I ask him, sun bright,
if he'd like to take a walk with me.
A new coffee shop just opened,
Starbucks, does he want to try it.

We walk, slowly, hand in hand,
to 87th and Broadway.
We get things called Venti Frappuccinos,
which sound ridiculous but taste delicious—
and I don't think about
who sees or doesn't see
his AIDS face.
I just sip sweet sips.

Dad talks about all the big businesses
taking over Manhattan:
Tower Records,
Banana Republic.
How we're living
in a changing city.
Then he says, smiling,
sun blasting through the windows,
and I'm alive to see it.

OVERLAPPING LIVES

April heads downtown
with James
to stuff envelopes for a GMHC mailing.

This time, I don't ask to join,
just tell her I'm coming, bring Dylan.

On a crowded 9 train,
we hang on to silver poles,
where so many fingerprints
have already left their mark.
Think about how many places
these people are going,
wonder how many to the
same street,
same building,
how many lives
are constantly overlapping.
Wonder if flutters of hope
(like mine)
can pass
from person to person
without so much
as a touch or
glance.

INSIDE OUR SELVES

I.
The Gay Men's Health Crisis sign
waves proudly in the breeze.

The mailing's in full swing.
Keith Haring posters everywhere,
men and women
talking over each other,
snacks and drinks.
Reminds me of a Yearbook meeting
except April, Dylan and I
are the only teenagers.
I wonder if any of these people
have children of their own.

I'm in charge of sticking address labels
on postcards.
I lay them out alphabetically,
pull them off delicately,
careful not to rip.
April licks the stamps.
Dylan stacks the postcards in messy piles,
shoos me away
when I start straightening them,
laughs, says *don't even think*
of micromanaging me.
April smiles.

II.

James knows everyone here.
Like he's in charge,
keeping things organized,
pouring Coke,
sneaking April extra Doritos.

Dylan talks about his cousin,
now suffering with pneumonia.

James shows us proofs
for new safe sex ads
for the buses and subways, asks
for our "youthful opinion."

As if James is so old?

April tells me James is here
almost all the time
when he's not teaching,
playing music,
caring for Dad.

I think about how our lives don't just overlap
with other people's, but how
inside each person
we are
so many selves
all at once.

MOVING THE AIR

In Peer Mentorship,
we discuss safe sex.
Condoms, pamphlets.

Mr. R introduces the topic,
then steps into the hall.
Two Freshmen blow condom balloons,
toss them back and forth.
Girls laugh.

Heat swells inside me.

I erupt:

My dad's dying from AIDS.

It's not just happening in Africa.

Condoms aren't a joke.

You need to be safe.

Their mouths hang open.

I'm sure they've heard the rumors
but it is different
to hear the truth spoken directly.

The condom balloons whiz to the ground.

And even though the windows are closed,

and the fans are turned off,

the air feels like it's moving.

THE BLANKET OF THE MOON

SOLAR ECLIPSE, MAY 10, 1994

Mr. Lamb leads us out
to watch the sky,
clutching our pinpricked cardboard
for the solar eclipse.

We herd across the street.
As the sky grows dark,
Dylan asks me—in a whisper—
if I want to go to prom with him.

I smile as
the always-lit New York City
goes dark for a bit
of day.

Moon and sun,
the same for the moment.

Together, light and dark, they make something
more beautiful than when alone:

A moon with sun's rays.
A sun the color of moon.

And then I tell Dylan
I'll go to prom with him

if he'll do something in return:
march alongside
me and my family
in the AIDS Walk.
For Dad, for his cousin.
I thought you'd never ask,
Dylan says, smiling,
hugging me,
just as the sun reemerges
from behind
the blanket of the moon.

FLYING

April and I walk
from school
to street corner
to store,
passing out
flyers
for the AIDS Walk.

We curve through the crowded blocks,
shoulder to shoulder,
stream through the streets.

Carol at the Starlight Diner
lets us put a stack
on the windowsill.

Chloe puts some up
in her own neighborhood.

The movie theater won't take the flyers.
Celestial Treasures does, of course.

Others fly away
in the early May winds.

The last place we hit
is Adam's lobby.

Put some in an envelope,
label it 11C.

I might never hear from Adam again,
so he might never know:
when he pushed me out

I floated
into the black
and found there
the light of my family and true friends.
And like a real North Star
it guided me home.

OUR OWN SKY RAINBOW

AIDS Walk, May 22, 1994

I.
On the way there
April chatters about the history
of the Walk:
it started in 1984,
San Francisco,
there are Walks everywhere now,
even in Kansas,
she says.
I listen,
wonder what it will feel like,
marching with so many people
affected,
infected,
by this disease,
wonder if anyone's story
is just like our own.

April and I meet up with Dylan,
join James, register walkers.
Hordes of people swarm
Central Park
with their papers.

A teenage girl, just my height,
comes to the table, pushing

a man in a wheelchair,
face and neck spotted with lesions.

Says she and her dad are here to register.
Her father looks much worse off than mine.
I wonder if she knows about astragalus,
pineapple juice, protein shots.
Wonder if she has anyone else to help
with her dying father.
Hand her the papers,
thank her for coming,
tell her it should be a great day.
She smiles weakly—
says *we need one of those.*

Next:
two men,
a couple,
arms locked.
One flirts with James,
says the volunteers are getting better and better looking.
James laughs, gives them their papers.
One rests his head on the other's shoulder.
Says he's already tired, the other says
they'll walk and rest.
Rest and walk.
They move on.

Some members of ACT UP
approach us with their own flyers,

I recognize the slogan:
SILENCE = DEATH.

For the first time
I think I know what this means.
How silence
breeds secrecy, shame.
How I hurt myself
being silent.
How silence can ruin
lives.

April and James speak Spanish
with an older woman,
who says she's here to march for
her son, who's in the hospital.

Chloe arrives,
wearing layers of rainbow clothes.

Birds tweet in trees,
the sun sits high in the sky,
masses of people ready to march,
spilling out
into the streets,
red ribbons on display,
they begin to cheer,
wave rainbow flags.

I look around and wonder how
I ever could have
thought myself
alone.

II.
We meet Mom,
who's pushing Dad
in a wheelchair of his own.
Waving a small flag.

We burst onto Central Park West,
turquoise sky sloping between
one building and the next,
walking north,
up, up,
we all take turns pushing Dad.

The sky splinters and darkens.
Volunteers pass out ponchos, Gatorade.
Mom puts Dad's hat on.
James grabs him a drink.

As we walk,
I see that girl again
with her father,
and I notice
another man with them now,
and a woman.
Flanking them.

She looks at me,
and sort of waves.
I sort of wave back.

Two families
in reflection.

III.
On Riverside,
past our own apartment building,
rain threatens but then
the sky settles back
into baby blue.

James shouting, *Fight back! Fight AIDS!*

We join in.
Dylan and Chloe compete
to see who can yell the loudest.

There's no rainbow in the sky

but I wave my flag high.

April grins,

holding her crystal necklace

into the sun,

where it splashes

its own tiny rainbow

onto my arm.

SUMMER

FIREWORKS

Last quarter moon,
Dad still hanging on.
Forty-two days longer than they said he would.
Can he make it longer still?
To graduation?
Beyond?
Open my Astro textbook,
search for an answer,
stare at photo after photo of nebulas.

They may only be gas shells
produced by dying stars—

a star's last wish—

but they look like
fireworks,
red, purple clouds

of hope—

                    a *yes*

suspended

in a wide-open

sky.

WATCH IT FLY

Yearbook's out.
Grab Chloe, to the stairwell,
flip through it together.

The front page quote, my idea, still reads:

When we look to the stars
we are looking back in time . . .

Cliques sit in star clusters,
faculty fly in rocket ships,
whole grades in constellations.

I'm not listed as editor,
or even on staff,
but my ideas
sparkle and light up
the pages.

I know, in a small way, I
helped make
something
lasting.

I carry a small rainbow flag in my pocket,
the one Dad held during the Walk.

Tell Chloe
I have to go
somewhere alone,
I'm okay.

When I get there,
use my old key.
Sit down at that long white counter.
Open the drawer.

Take a minute to
sort the paper clips
from the tacks
from the erasers.

Then, go to the yearbooks,
and next to the spine of the 1976 edition,
I stick in the tiny flag.

Watch the rainbow

throw its color all over

that white room.

IN A FLASH

Prom night.
Put up my hair.
Put my dangly earrings on.
Step into my blue dress.

Dad says I look like a mermaid.
Mom takes pictures.

The mirror, like a camera,
freezes time in a flash,
catching all of us
inside of it
for one brief
moment.

ORION'S BELT

I.
Last year,
on the dance floor,
I twirled in,
Adam spun me out.

Tonight, I focus on Dylan.
Notice for the first time
a Saturn ring of yellow
surrounding the soft brown
of his eyes.

II.
At the after-prom party,
Adam and I
kept to ourselves.
We sipped Sprite,
toasted to summertime
while everyone else
cheered and clinked
glasses of champagne.

Tonight we take a limo
to a classmate's beach house.
On the way—Dylan's hand
on my leg, casually, like it's always
been there. Chloe, in a pink slip dress,

with some new guy
who seems nicer than the others.

The air's just warm enough
to roll down the windows,
stars blinking at us all the way
to the beach.

III.

My head spins
as Dylan and I lie
back in the grass
on the front lawn.

Dylan draws
small circles
on my inner
wrist.

*My dad's lived
six weeks more
than they said he would.*

I say it twice.

The second time
a tear rolls down
my cheek.

He kisses

it

away.

Pointing up to the sky,
he traces Orion's Belt
with his finger,

I grab it
when it comes back down.

He draws me in,
I don't pull away.

BIRDS IN PARADISE

The next day,
high heels in hand,
Dylan's tux jacket on,
home to find
Mom and Dad
in the living room,
sewing machine out.

Him hunched over it, stitching.
Her in a sea of fabrics
and feathers.

Mom said they decided
to make a costume together.
Just for fun.

I watch Dad press his foot on the pedal.
I watch Mom cut.

They argue over the true hue of chartreuse.
Laugh about the thunderstorm during the parade the year
        they met.

They work for hours.
April helps me make dinner.

When they're done,
a mask of petals,
tail of stems,
Dad says it isn't their finest work.
Mom agrees.
But I think it is.

RECORDING SESSION

SESSION EIGHT

Okay, Dad, it's almost graduation.
Seven whole weeks past—

      Doomsday.

Yeah.

So time for some real serious questions.

      Uh-oh.

What's the best meal you ever ate?

      (Laughs)
      Probably one I had in Italy one summer with your
      mother before you were born. It was the kind of meal
      that went on for hours.

What about your happiest childhood memory?

      My mama teaching me to sew.

The time you felt most proud of yourself?

The day I was accepted to college.

And it's almost your turn now.

No rush.

Not yet.

Nope—first you have to walk the stage.

(Long pause)

Dad, why are you crying?

Don't worry, honey. These are happy tears.

ENDINGS ARE BEGINNINGS

I stand in a sea of black,
a group of graduates,
of smiles and sweat,
lining up,
marching forward, under
the brightest lights.

Chloe salutes me, flashes her Vans.
Dylan half smiles at me, I smile back.
We, the class of 1994,
face
the crowd.

A big-deal news reporter talks
about the opportunity
to go forth unafraid, follow your future,
trust your path, make
your way,

look back on this time and remember it was special.
Her voice floats away like
a drifting log

and all I can see is him:

smiling large,
bright blue eyes
focused right on me.

Dad Is Here.

I exhale deep as
he lifts his long, thin arm
and waves.

NEVER LETS GO

A few nights later,
Chloe and I
meet up with some other
girls from our class.
She wants us to try
to get into a dance club
to celebrate our independence.

Skirt flowing,
letting Chloe put toffee lipstick on me
when the phone rings.

Mom:

Dad
back in the hospital.

Chloe
forgets the club,
hails the cab,
comes to the hospital
and even though we aren't dancing
she never lets go of my hand.

IN TUBES

April meets me in the lobby,
face wet, says he's in Intensive Care,
I tell Chloe to go,
I'll call with updates.

The fluorescent light
coats us, Dad back in tubes,
all of us in masks.

The monitor beeps.

Mom puts her hand on my back.

Pneumonia,

she says.

THE SOUND OF IT

Home for a few hours,
then in the morning,
back at the hospital.

James steps out,
gives April and me some time.
Mom spent the night last night,
asks if I want a turn.

Dad's moved from Intensive Care
to a private room.
If it weren't for his diaper, the IVs,
it could almost seem like a hotel.

I place an amethyst on his chest,
he smiles,
curls his fingers around it.

Says when he dies, he wants a party.
Nothing sad, he says, a celebration of life.

I tell him *shhh,*
ask if he wants to watch TV.
Hoarsely, he whispers
put on something brilliant.

Lucky for us,
Amadeus is on.

Mozart's hands speeding
over the piano keys
as Salieri seethes
with jealousy.

Dad tries to conduct
a few times with his hands
but they are attached to
too many things.
A nurse comes in,
asks him to not move around
so much.

The credits roll as Mozart
releases his last
high-pitched cackle
over the screen's darkness.

Dad laughs too.

I imagine the sound echoing

through the hospital hallways,

shaking the pill bottles

right off that nurse's tray.

DECLARATION

The doctor says
there's nothing more anyone can do.
He made it longer than they expected.

She's sending him home *to be comfortable*, she says.

Though none of us say it,
his wheezing, coughing, skeletal body

shows us

what she really means.

CHECKMATE

Back in my parents' bedroom.

Dad asks me to promise

I will take a road trip someday.

Drive it all by myself.

That I will learn to play chess.

I say I promise;

he closes his eyes.

I lie down next to him.

For this moment,

we are both

still and

breathing.

THROUGH WINDOWS

April and I take turns
spooning Dad broth
from a blue ceramic bowl.

No more herbs.
No more custard apple.
Crystals just sitting
on the windowsill,
blinking their light.

No more Gloria,
just hospice workers.

Other teens at the beach,
tanning, flipping magazines.

April and I home,
feeding Dad:

The only sun
on our faces
sliced in
through
half-open
windows.

FROM DULL TO LIGHT

We all go to him.

His eyes move from dull
to light
when I tell him
we made something

all of us—together—

for him.

I press play.

What do you love about Dad? I ask.

Mom answers:

>   *His generosity. His belief in second chances.*

And April:

>   *The way he used to tuck me in.*
>   *Made me feel safe.*

Me:

>   *How he hums while he cooks.*

And James:

His laugh. So deep and contagious.

Mom:

His creative spirit.

April:

How he'll talk to anyone on the street.

Me:

How he always knows his opinion.

James:

He lectures and people listen.

Mom:

His creations.

April:

How excited he gets about what he loves.

Me:

> *How he's always been there for me.*

What will you miss most about Dad?

April:

> *I will miss his hugs.*

Mom:

> *I will miss his smile.*

James:

> *I will miss his eyes.*

Me:

> *I will miss his voice.*

I shut off the tape.
All of us crying,
Dad telling us
not to worry,

all four of us

at once.

MORPHINE DREAMS

We take turns sitting with him,
the next few days.
Doped up on morphine,
his words cut
from a collage of dreams:

Stir the gravy—quick!

               Your mother, with wings.

Marching, lights from sequins.

         She was born with her arms open.

Red to purple to white.

             A party in the street.

              Class, turn to page 35.

          Wondrous creatures—

COMA

In Astronomy,
a coma is the glowing gas cloud
around
the comet's nucleus.
At home,
a coma is something Dad has
fallen into.

Holding his cold hand

watching his

heavy shell of a body

drag breaths
wondering

what's still   inside of him

what has already   floated up
and out.

I want to scream
I'm sorry.

Sorry for wasting   so much time.

Not being with him.

Sorry for not   being more forgiving.

Not ready   to say goodbye.

Not knowing how   this kind of pain

ever   floats away.

THROUGH TEARS

James says his goodbye first.

He carries *Don Quixote*.
He blasts *La Traviata*.

April and I watch a *90210* repeat,
try not to listen.

When he comes out,
April says
she's so sorry
the herbs,
the plan
didn't work.

James says,
through tears,

It worked—

as much as anything could have.

He takes something from his pocket,
pours some water.
Moves hand to mouth quickly.
Swallows.

Selenium.

GATHERING

Flip off the TV.
Listen:
April's goodbye.
Look out the window
at all that new green life.
She tells him in English,
then in Spanish,
she won't give up fighting.

When she leaves the room,
I gather her in my arms,
limb over limb,
run my hand through
her new short hair,
realize that
when I wasn't looking
she sprouted inches
taller than me.

THROUGH GASPS

Linger in the doorway,
listen:

Mom's goodbye.

She holds their flower costume
like a child and her blankie.

Talks about their Bermuda vacation,
white sands, turquoise water,
how they held each other on that beach
for hours. How tall he was, strong.

She says:

I will do my best to take care of these girls—
our girls—
the way you did, Dale.

Then, she says—

through gasps—

she will think of him
and try harder.

Dad's raspy breath
uneven now.

I walk back through the hall,
sign my name with my finger

on the cold, white wall.

SPINNING CLOUD OF LIGHT

White sheets contain his coma.
I hold his legs, cry into them
until there's nothing left of me,
let out all that I've been keeping in.
Match his dragging breaths.

In a spinning cloud of light

I promise him:

I will create something
of meaning.

I will add to the story.

I will ask for help when I need it.
I will not stay silent.

I say goodbye.

THE NEUTRAL, YELLOW
DARK

Candlelight floats over the bed.
New Jersey skyline blinks
out the window.

Dad lets out his last breath.

I kneel at his body.
Mom and James
decide to keep him all night.

A thin strip
of white moon
hides behind a building.

April and I sleep—

curled into each other
like puppies.

SILVER, EMPTY

The next day
we stare at
Dazed and Confused,
Sixteen Candles.
The undertakers go in and out
of my parents' bedroom.
They speak softly,
finally
carry him out
in a black body bag.

I think about
the hallway mirror,
a silent, sturdy witness:

It's seen
Dad making costumes,
helping us with our homework,
me sneaking in late,
fighting,

now
the mirror—
reflecting, empty—
watches
him go.

WHAT'S FALLING

I dream.

I enter the bus.
I see him.
He's in my regular seat,
wrapped in a brown, fur-lined coat.
Thin blond hair matted against his head.
He could have been somebody, I think.
I sit next to him,
feel him shiver.
His head bent forward.
I can see now, he's hiding something.
I ask him what he has.
He shakes his head no.
Bites his chapped lips.
Whole body starts to tremble.
I think about pulling the emergency cord—
no one else notices he's shaking.
There's a man in a suit. A baby on a lap.
Preteen girls playing MASH.
Someone listening to a Walkman loudly.

Why can't they see him?

His body shakes, I try and hold him still.
But he's too big. Too long. Items fall
from his coat.

A diploma.
A poem.
A chess piece.
A feather.
I pick them up, stuff them into
my backpack. His whole body now
shaking, trembling, dying.
There's nothing to do but
collect what's falling.
A tie.
A bead.
A slotted spoon.
A sandwich.

I say loudly,
to deaf ears:
He could have been someone.

I yell until the bus stops.
I wake up screaming.

SOMETHING SOLID

The wake.
His mouth's been stuffed.
It looks all wrong.

Like a B actor cast
to play my father.

I dare myself to touch his face.
It feels like wood,

or colder,
like glass.

Chloe gets me some food,
I pick at it.

I think about Dylan.
About Existentialism.

All those philosophers saying there's
nothing out there to believe in.

And how making something meaningful
was so important to my dad.

But now he's gone.
Now, he's the nothing.

Dylan shows up, as if he knows
I'm thinking about him.

He takes my hand.
I let myself lean into him.

To feel something warm.

The crowd swells
and he knows

I need to leave it.
He pulls me to
the coats and we huddle
under them.

We don't kiss.
We don't even talk.
We just play hangman.

He names the category:

Space.

NOTHINGNESS

So many people attend the funeral.
Our teachers, his students,
neighbors, friends.

Chloe points out Adam,
standing with his parents,
they sneak out the back
as soon as it's over.
I greet the others person by person,
kiss cheeks,
nod, say thanks
when people say sorry.

After everyone leaves,
April, Chloe, Dylan and I
gather the programs
left behind,
scattered like this was a play—
a concert—abandoned
just after the encore.

At home,
I stack the programs neatly.
Try to iron out the creases
left
on the copies of his face.

NIGHTTIME

We went to Zabar's earlier and bought
Brie
caviar
Carr's crackers—
what Dad would've bought himself.

We host a party.
As requested.

But now, "celebrating" with all these people,
my friends smoking in the stairwell,
his friends playing the piano, drinking,
the world wobbles beneath me.

All I can think to do
is lie on his side
of my parents' bed.

That night:
I dream Dad is dancing,
like he can hear our music,
under a spinning disco ball,
and in his own way
he keeps the time.

THE MAN IN THE MOON

I bathe in moon.

I find the man
carved into its face.
I can't stop looking.

Cracked smile.
Deep well eyes.

How does he feel hovering
in this starless New York City sky?

I get lost in caverns of gray space.

From the window
of my bathroom,
looking out onto the Hudson,

wonder how it could seem so peaceful
but hold so much junk.

I light candles.
Spin circles in water.

I no longer count time,
days tick by.

ON REPEAT

A week later,
light blinking
over and over
on my answering machine.

Gloria, checking in.
Chloe, asking me to take the Jitney
to the Hamptons,
just for the night,
some big party.
James asks if April and I
want to meet for coffee.
Dylan plays me Phish.
My college roommate
asks when can we talk.

I delete everything but the songs.
Those I play on repeat.

ALMOST

Mom, in the kitchen crying.

I put my hand on her shoulder,

ask if she wants to cook something.

She says she doesn't know how.

I hand her an apron.

Show her how to dice the onions, Dad's way.

April joins us midway.

She opens cans of beans, tomatoes.

All three of us make Dad's chili.

We get it—almost—right.

We take our time eating.

April adds extra salt.

Mom reheats hers in the microwave.

As we finish up,

the summer sun lingering

late into the night,

I ask Mom if I

can go with her

to her studio

tomorrow.

HOLDING NEPTUNE

I.
Walking in
feels like entering a memory.
The last time I was here
was for one of Mom's shows,
years ago,
before she left for Italy.

April comes too, we're outsiders in the hot shop.
Glassblowers share the huge studio space.
A warehouse of furnaces burning molten glass.
Artists work in teams, taking turns
dipping their rods,
then blowing into them.
Mom's the gaffer today,
she leads her team.
We follow her.
She gathers
the yellow-red glowing glass
onto her torch.

The heat so hot it stings my face,
I almost have to turn away.

Mom faces the fire.

Says hi to some guy named Larry,
another named Ron.

Everyone here seems to know her.
Respect her.

A fat man at the next station pulls
white-and-red liquid glass like taffy.
A younger guy snips it into pieces
like huge peppermint candies.

It's like a circus,
Mom, the ringleader.

II.
Before we start
making our own art,
she tells us
about Wabi-Sabi,
the Japanese practice of
putting a thumbprint
on every piece you create
to show it is human-made,
imperfection makes it beautiful.

She says this is how she approaches her own art,
and this is how she approaches life too,
something made,
imperfect by design.

I shield Mom's glass with the paddle
as she spins the rod,
an artist named Rose blows through it.

Mom says that every piece starts as a sphere.

No matter what you're making.

She asks if I want a turn.

I gaze at the glowing torch.

Nod, take Rose's place.

Mom guides me, says to blow into the rod.

Tells me my breath's too shallow,

she says to use all my force.

I fight the impulse to give up.

The rod burns my lips as it spins

but I keep trying—blowing harder—

until the glowing blue sphere grows.

It veers sideways,
not at all like the round bubbles
Mom blew before.

Lopsided.

Asymmetrical.

I tell her I want to do it again.
I want to try to make it perfect, round.

She says
art

is not about

perfection.

Remember Wabi-Sabi.

III.
Later, we carry the bubble down the winding halls
to her workstation.

I gasp—
a whole solar system is hanging.

She tells me we are holding Neptune.
Says it's the last planet to add.
Says it's for me, for my dorm room.

We hang my imperfect Neptune
where it belongs,
the solar system rattles,

and settles into something beautiful.

AS HIMSELF

I wander the apartment
in Dad's Texas T-shirt.
Flick on the TV.
Off.
Microwave water for ramen.
On/off.
Keep expecting to see Dad.
It's been almost a month now
but still
I hear him say:

Mira, ramen is not real food. It's dorm food.
Speaking of which, we need to buy you
new sheets for college. Shower shoes.

Some days I hear him pour oil into the pan.
It sizzles.
Smell onions, carrots, peppers.
I hear him cough,
hear his footsteps,
hear him cry at Hallmark commercials.

Other days, I hear him make dinner conversation.
He asks what I'll be for Halloween this year.
I tell him I don't know yet.

He laughs.
Says:

This year, for Halloween, Miranda?
I'm going as myself.

I tell him April and I saw *Forrest Gump*
four times in one week.
That he would have loved it,
how Forrest runs and runs
across America.
How Jenny dies at home
with her family.
He says:

Sounds like our kind of movie.

I tell him I've been teaching Mom to cook,
about my college roommate assignment.

I tell him that April has taken up running in the park.

That Mom took us to the studio, made me a
mobile, told us about Wabi-Sabi:

And that maybe,
just like art,
we are something made, not perfect.

I tell him that I miss him.

That I will learn to play chess, take a road trip someday.

Then, one day, the house is quiet.
I hear the front door open and
I hear him say *goodbye*.

CUT FROM SKY

The doorbell rings,
James is there.
For the first time I notice
his eyes—
the same bright blue
as Dad's—circles cut from sky.

He tells me Mom asked him to help her
sort some of Dad's teaching files.

I ask him—
because Mom hardly knows how—
if, after we're done, he could take me
out in the family car.

Give me a lesson.

He arches his eyebrows,
a new piercing hangs from one.

He says to wait
just a minute—
he'll get the keys—
we'll do that first.

Driving sounds a lot more fun than filing.

BLIND SPOTS

James pulls the car around the corner.

My stomach lurches.

He switches to the passenger side—

Me, the driver.

James shares the secret to driving well:
not just having awareness of other people
but believing you, yourself,
are in control.

I nod.

He turns on the radio.

"Alex Chilton" by the Replacements starts playing.

I drive down West End,

windows down, we both hum along.

Twenty minutes later,
up and around the neighborhood,
he tells me I'm ready for the highway.

I say *but there are so many people—*

he says *they want to live too.*

I can't help but laugh.

Turn left on 79th.

Back to the Henry Hudson, 9A.

When I merge onto the highway,
a red car honks at me loudly,
then swerves into another lane.

James tells me it's okay,
that was my blind spot.

I make it four more exits,
staying in the right lane,
without another person honking at me.
A smile breaks from my lips.

For the first time in weeks, I feel something—possibility.

I tell him *Dad always said you were a good teacher.*

He says he heard I was a good student.

I ask if we can do it again,

if he thinks I could pass my test
before I leave for school.

He says
he knows I can
if we practice
every day.

We park and take the elevator up,

me with a smile.

James in my peripheral vision,

still humming "Alex Chilton,"

and I realize that blind spots

aren't just

about driving.

STARSHELLS

I.
That night, Chloe and Dylan kidnap me,
take me to the ocean.

They have a surprise, they say.

In Chloe's Volvo,
I stretch my dad's T-shirt
over my knees.

Chloe tells me I need to change clothes,
there's no excuse for bad hygiene.

I can't see the ocean
but, with the window down,
I can smell, almost taste,
the salt.

II.
They bought me a telescope.

We watch stars firework across the night.
Up close, like Mr. Lamb's slides.

I stargaze,
Dylan hugs me from behind.

He kisses me once,
Chloe turns cartwheels
in the sand.

Pieces of shell glint
all around us,
like thousands of stars
rained to Earth.

I gather one for each of them.

A deep blue mussel for Chloe.

For Dylan, a heart-shaped cockle.

For James, two shiny jingles.
Mom, a soft white slipper shell.

Rainbow-striped scallop for April.

Angel's wings
for Dad.

And for me,

a
Venus clam.

WITH CAUTION

Two more weeks of daily lessons,
on busy streets, the highway,
one week left before school starts,
James says it's time.
His eyes gloss over.
I wonder
if missing someone feels the same
inside every person.

Ride the subway uptown,
enter a tan box of a building.
For the first time,
I say a prayer—
for Dad to keep me
safe.

During the test,
I brake with caution,
keep my hands at 10 and 2.
Park as best I can,
tricky, imperfect.
Relax a little and
let the road lead me.

After the test, the instructor pauses for a minute,
scratches his head, sighs, says
I need to work on

my parallel parking.
He also says *congratulations.*

I emerge, excited, relieved,
look for Dad.

And then I remember.
Again.

For the first time, I notice James's face thinning,
his muscles weakening.
I let him,
with his sleeves of tattoos,
new eyebrow piercing,

put his arm around me.
He says
Your dad would be so proud.

And I know he's right.

REPAIRED, IN PLACES

Before I leave for college,

I decide to fix Mom's glass fish.

Bring it to Gloria, ask if she can help.

She has just the thing,

leads me to the back of the store.

Clamps.
Epoxy glue.

Tells me it will take a few minutes.

We fit tail
to fin
to head.

While she works,

I thank her for all she did for our family.

How even though he died,
she gave us much-needed time.

She smiles,
tells me to visit her
when I return.

When she's finished,

the fish doesn't look perfect,

but it's whole again—

scarred,

and repaired, in places.

TAKEOFF

Chloe doesn't leave until next week.
I promise to meet her over break.
Together again, with our fake IDs.

Dylan makes me a mixtape for school.
We promise to write.
Maybe try this new thing, AOL.

Mom packages up the glass
solar system for my dorm room.
James helps me carry my stuff—
telescope,
big trunk,
a duffel—
to the sidewalk.

Don't know if I'm ready
for another goodbye.
Even a temporary one.
Mom drops something into my hand.
I feel the ridges, the weight—
keys.
Tears float into my eyes.
My heart swells like the moon.

Mom says *Dad wanted you to have this*.
James nods, says the car is mine.

April, in her new ACT UP T-shirt,
curls her arms around me,
rests her head on my shoulder.
Mom smiles.

All at once I know
I have to make this drive myself.

Mom says she and April
will visit soon
for Parents' Weekend.
We hug goodbye.

I climb into the driver's seat,
wave to April, Mom and James,
together, on the corner.

Check my mirrors,
turn onto the Henry Hudson,
the steering wheel glides
gently under my fingers,
Dylan's mix on loud,
Rusted Root blasts as
I leave the edge of Manhattan—

Roll down the window,
shout goodbye
to my windowseat,
goodbye to the Big Rock.

A crystal hangs from the rearview mirror.
A map by my side.

The road,
solid
beneath me

as I blast into

the summer-gold
sky.

Written with pride
in honor of
my father
Kenneth Philip Allen
1938–1994

Acknowledgments

As is stated by many VCFA authors, this book would not exist without my experience at Vermont College of Fine Arts and, specifically, the talented teachers I had the honor of working with: Coe Booth, Mary Quattlebaum, Julie Larios and An Na. Thank you for loving Mira back when she was Lia and even farther back when she was me. Special thanks to Coe for her incredible support after graduation as well. Thank you to the Secret Gardeners, especially the wildly creative, smart and perceptive Laura Sibson, Laurie Morrison, Mary Winn Heider and Miriam McNamara. I cherish you. Special thanks to Melanie Crowder and Skila Brown for verse novel support, positivity, encouragement.

Sara Crowe, thank you for working so hard to bring this book to life and being so present during the hard times. Your energy is inspiring. Liza Kaplan, Editor Extraordinaire, you are perhaps the most conscientious person I've ever encountered (Mira would like to study under you). Thank you for all the brainstorming, all the nitpicking, all the pushing and the praise. Thank you for that day on the phone, when you told me you were meant to find my story. One of the best days of my life; I owe you the moon. Much thanks to the Philomel constellation: Michael Green, Talia Benamy, Kristin Smith, Semadar Megged, Cindy Howle, John Searcy and Ryan Sullivan. Your hard work means so much to me. This book should have all your names on the cover.

Thank you to my writer friends named Dan: Dan Torday, you are the one who first got on me to go back to school, and your long-standing belief in me means so much; Dan Boehl, thank you for alternating challenge/support, for TIE in the face of TFO and for all those mixtapes. Thanks to my many "Philly mom friends" who listened to me talk on and on about this process and who loved my family and me through it; you know who you are. Special thanks to Jenna Conley for lending her HIV expertise to the story. Lots of love always to my badass friend and glassblowing expert, Erica Rosenfeld. And to Vanessa Brown Sughrue, for being such a caring friend and a good listener. Thanks to Beth Ann Corr, for being an amazing acupuncturist; you helped me through some stuck moments. And Lisa Marchiano, for empowerment.

This book was a long time coming. A long, long time ago it was a memoir. Some of the images included I can trace back to poems I wrote during undergrad at Kenyon. Although the book was once a true story, it is now, *absolutely*, a work of fiction. That being said, I thought so much about my own childhood/high school experience as I wrote this, and the experience of losing my own father to AIDS. I thought so much about some people (even though none appear directly in the book) who journeyed alongside me during that time and who, as I wrote, would poke their heads into my office sometimes, say hi, hold my hand, shed a tear. For this, I thank the memories of my own star cluster: Kiki Samuels, Freya Wallace, Kendall Wishnick Adams, Jana Gold Kleiman, Eliza Nemser, Laura Kleger, David Hong, Jeremy Kleiner, Xander Charity, Matt Ross, Josh Melnick. And David Lowy, thanks for being so nice to me back then. Thanks to the Longacre summer program and the friends I made there, specifically Susan Smith, for teaching me the power of openness. Thanks so much to my Nana, Lillian Allen, for teaching me what it means to love unconditionally. Endless thanks to Joan McAllister for taking such good care of me my whole life. I thank my mother, Mariette Pathy Allen, for supporting me throughout this process and lovingly answering so many hard questions. A thousand million tons of love to my best, taller and better-than-me little sister, Julia Steele Allen. You are as precious as you are courageous. I love you 4eva. To Jon Jensen, my heroic, dashing husband, who literally sat through twenty thousand sessions of me reading this book out loud, I do not have words for you. I do not know how to thank you enough for supporting me tirelessly. I love you. And my darling, amazing children, Lily and Tate: I love you all the time, you are my best, best ones. You guys are the absolute coolest. I want to be both of you when I grow up.